CW00871738

Huckleberry

An American Story

by

M.M. Riley

Copyright 2005 Megan Riley McGilchrist

All rights reserved.

For L, J, & K

Chapter One

Huckleberry. It's a funny name for a man, I know. I reckon Pap thought it was a good joke, or maybe it's the kind of pie Ma made the day I was born. I'm sure Pap wouldn't a let her lie around in bed for long. Anyway, I've been called a lot of other things, but mainly I just answer to Huck now. I've already written something about what my life was like growing up, all the silly things me and Tom Sawyer did when we was boys together, so I guess I'll take up where I left off.

After all those shenanigans with Jim, the nigger we freed when he was already free, Aunt Sally, she did adopt me. I thought about runnin' off for awhile, but Aunt Sally and Uncle Silas was so nice to me, and they were old and all, and said I was like the boy they'd had that'd died of the swamp fever, and the kids were nice, and after awhile, I got used to it. They had a place just over the line in Louisiana, so I was a long way from home. And after Tom Sawyer and Jim went home, I have to say, I was pretty lonesome at first. And it was hot too, most all the time. And if it weren't hot it was rainin', but I got used to that too. And whenever I got too lonesome, I'd just mosey on over to the river and watch them steamers piling their way up north. Seeing them and knowing they were going back where I'd come from made me feel a little better somehow. And Aunt Sally and Uncle Silas treated me just like one of their own, and pretty soon, I forgot that I wasn't, so I have to say, it was a pretty comfortable life, even with school and church. I stood it, just.

And then one afternoon after I'd been there about seven or eight months, something happened. If you remember my other book, you'll remember about the King and the Duke, them rascals, and that nice family the Wilkses, up in Arkansas that those two tried to rob. Their Pa had died and the family was waiting for the old man's brothers to come out from England, and the King and the Duke, which warn't either one of 'em nothin' but carpet-bagging thieves, got wind of it when they was traveling with me and my runaway nigger, Jim, and they pretended to be the brothers. Well, it all come right in the end, but we had to high-tail it out of there, but not before I'd put Mary-Jane, one of the daughters, wise to the business.

Somehow, Mary-Jane had got wind of where I was and had heard what happened to the King and the Duke (last I saw 'em, they was covered with tar and feathers) and had come down to Louisiana to find me and say thanks. Well, Mary-Jane, she was the prettiest girl I ever saw, and like I said before, she had the most sand of any girl I ever knew. I wasn't more than thirteen when I was going down the river with Jim, and to be honest, no one was ever too sure how old I was, Pap not havin been one for throwing birthday parties. But in the time I'd been with Aunt Sally and Uncle Silas, I'd growed up quite a lot. I even had to borrow uncle Silas's razor once or twice a week, and I was a head taller than Tom Sawyer. Mary-Jane, she must've been nineteen or twenty, thereabouts. Anyway, when she run me down, I was powerful glad to see her, gladder than I thought I should be, if you know what I mean. Well, she stayed with us about a week, and she wanted to give me a reward for what I'd done, but I said there warn't no need, since I was rich already - that was cause of the treasure that me and Tom Sawyer found in Injun Joe's cave. That's in the other book too. So I told her to keep her money for her and her sisters, but I'd be mighty obliged if I could come and call on them one day if I was traveling north. She wrote me a few letters, after she went home, kind of sisterly-like, but I didn't write back more n' once or twice, not being much hand at writin'.

Well, what with school and learning how to be a Phelps, and helpin' on the farm, I almost forgot about Mary-Jane till one day when I was about seventeen and I'd been with Aunt Sally and Uncle Silas for near on four years. Aunt Sally had got a letter from her sister Aunt Polly, who Tom Sawyer lived with, saying why didn't we all come for a visit. Well Aunt Sally, she hummed and hawed and fussed and fidgeted about it for a week or more, and finally she said, why didn't I go. I was old enough to take a river trip by myself and it'd be nice for me to see all my old friends, and so on. Well, I jumped at the chance. It seemed like I never knowed how much I missed Missouri till I got a chance to go back. So it was all decided and I got on that riverboat the next Saturday looking like a real gentleman - I was over six feet by then, and shaving every day - not like the little torn-britches kid that had come down the river four years before on a raft with a runaway slave. And I was dressed smart too, or smart for those parts. I'd got used to good clothes by then, and they didn't bother me like they used to when I was runnin' wild.

Well, that riverboat trip, it was fine. There ain't nothin' like the old Mississippi, grand and fierce, but peaceful and quiet too. We'd pass other boats goin' south, and rafts like the one me and Jim had been on. The people on the other boats would wave to us and we'd wave back like we was old friends meetin' in a new place. And when the boat stopped to take on passengers or drop off freight or people, you never seen such goings-on. Sometimes we'd pull up to'ards some little river town, just dozin' in the midday sun. As soon as the whistle she blows, you could see the whole place spring to life. You could see wagons and carts comin' towards the wharf, and people hustling up with cases and boxes. And the town boys runnin' to the edge and 'most pushin' each other in, and sometimes pushin' each other in, and climbin' out and chasin' and fightin', and the dogs barkin' and the mothers of them boys screamin' at 'em to get away, the boat's a-comin' and the wheel could drag 'em down. And here comes the boat, grand as she can be, and all them in the town just stoppin' and starin', like I would a done if I'd been one of 'em. And lots goin' on on the boat too. All the folks gettin' off millin' around, deckhands ready with ropes to tie her up when she gets close enough, steam screamin', water rushin round the bow and churnin' at the back, then the wheel stops and she docks. Then such comin's and goings people crowdin' up and crowdin' down that gangway. Hands haulin' stuff up and down. Ropes and pulleys swingin'. Then just like that, it's over. The boat steams up, the ropes are hauled off and coiled up, and in a minute that little town is disappearin' behind the wake. A couple of dogs will be barkin' on the wharfside, and the boys will run along the river bank shoutin' till they get snagged by a tree trunk, or a stream stops 'em, and they go back home and drink lemonade and talk about it until the next one comes through.

I spent a lot of time talking to the pilot. He told me about how you'd got to know the river upstream, and downstream, and how that was like two differn't rivers, and how you'd got to know it at night as well as day, and that was like two more. By jingo, he knew ever' inch of that river, all four of 'em, and every spar and landin' stage all the way from New Orleans to Cincinnati. I figured maybe I'd go to work on a river boat one day. But things didn't turn out that way, not at all, like you'll see when I get to that part of the story. Sometimes I'd just hang over the edge looking out for places I remembered that me and Jim had seen when we was on our trip on the raft. I recognized a lot of 'em, and figured maybe piloting a boat wouldn't be so hard after all. There's somethin' real peaceful 'bout bein' on a river, even in a great big boat like that one was. Kind of like time she stands still and you just sort of pass over it. Then one morning I heard the engine slowing up and we stopped at a place that looked real familiar. There was some people getting on and suddenly I remembered it. By jingo, it was the place where the King and the Duke had tried to pretend they was Peter Wilks's brothers and rob the family of their fortune, and damned if it wasn't Mary-Jane Wilks a-gettin' on the boat!

Well I ran down there as fast as I could and as Mary-Jane put her foot on the deck I just about hollered, "Mary-Jane! How are ya!" Well she looked at me real funny for a minute, then her face it changed and it was just like the sun coming out of a fogbank, and she said, "Huckleberry Finn! I'd of known you anywhere, but look how grown up you are!" Well, ever'body on the boat was a lookin' at us and smiling, and the people on the landing, they were smiling too cause Mary-Jane called down to them, "Look who's here, Huckleberry Finn, who saved the family!" Well I felt pretty good after that especially when Mary-Jane she paid so much attention to me. She was about twenty-three by then, and pretty! Well, I never seen a girl grow into such a nice, growed up looking woman, and no airs, neither. She was just as nice to me as if I was her brother, and pretty near the rest of the trip we had our dinners together and walked on the deck and talked. She could talk! But not like some girls, not silly things that she knew a fella wouldn't understand, like about dresses and such, no she talked about all kinds of things, history and politics, all kinds of stuff. That girl knew more stuff than any man or woman I'd ever known, and it wasn't just facts, she had opinions on everything she read. She knew about animals and birds too, and was quite a hand at bird-watchin'. Why sometimes we'd stand on deck for an hour or more just lookin' at all the birds near the shore, or flyin' round in the wake, and Mary-Jane, she knew the name of ever' one of them. She'd read most books ever written, I reckon. She was on her way to St. Louis, and then to England. She was a goin' to visit them real uncles, the ones that had come for Peter Wilks's funeral just in time to get rid of our gang.

Well, the night before we were getting to St. Louis, her and me, we were walking on the deck. The stars were out, and the boat was making that nice swooshing noise it does when the water's smooth, and it was a nice night. I kept looking out at the shore, cause we was in Missouri now, and I knowed it all good. I felt like I was goin' home, for sure, and I was tellin' Mary-Jane all about the folks I was goin' to see and the things we'd do. I was lookin' forward to seeing Tom Sawyer, specially. Well, Mary-Jane, she was real quiet, and then she finally said, "It certainly has been nice getting to know you again Huck."

And I felt kind of choked up when she said that, and I wanted to say somethin' nice to her, but all I could manage was, "Well, when you come back, come on down to visit us. I know Aunt Sally would be real happy to have you anytime."

She got kind of quiet then, and she said, "Well, I won't be coming back for awhile. I'm getting married."

Married! Well, I was just about blowed over the railings, but I recollected my schooling at Aunt Sally's just enough to say, "Congratulations. I hope you'll be very happy." I don't think Tom Sawyer himself could of managed that one much better.

And then she began to sniffle, and then she began wailing properly and she put her face in my shirt and just cried like a baby. I didn't know what to do, so I put my arms around her and before I knew what I was doin', I kissed her!

Then the whole story come out. After the uncles had gone home, they sent over one of their sons, and him and Mary-Jane kind of come to an arrangement, and it was all decided that she'd go back and marry him and live in Sheffield, England, and that's where she was going.

"Kind of funny," I said, "going back there when the whole world seems to want to come <u>here</u>."

Well that got her crying more, and I just didn't know what to do. And I guess she would've gone, if that storm hadn't of blowed up. In the middle of the night, I heard the old boat just creaking and wailing, and the wind howling. I hadn't gone to sleep at all, I'd been lyin' in my bunk thinkin' about Mary-Jane and wishin' she wasn't goin' away. I got dressed real quick and went up on deck to have a look. That storm had blowed up mighty quick, and she was a killer. The waves was already lashing and I reckoned it was too rough for the pilot to make the shore safely, so I figured he was just going to ride her out. You couldn't see nothing ten feet ahead nor ten feet behind of the boat and suddenly, I heard this almighty thump. I knew what that meant, so I run downstairs to Mary-Jane's cabin. There was people running around and screaming, and by the time I got to her, I thought we was goners. Mary-Jane, she was all dressed and sitting on her trunk. When I pulled the door open, she said, "I thought you'd never get here," and started dragging that trunk out.

"Leave that trunk," I near shouted, and she did. We just ran, and by the time we'd fought our way out to the top, that boat, she was turning turtle. "Can you swim?" I asked her. "Yes, some," she said.

"Well, jump!" And it was a good thing we did. We wasn't too far from the shore, and I never let go of her, but when I looked back I saw that boat all broke up on the shoal and people just howling in the water and getting dragged towards the wheel, and it was still turning.

We was damn near drowned, but we made it. When we got to shore, we watched that wreck, and saw people screamin' and drownin', and not a thing we could do. We was both soaked and shakin' and Mary-Jane was cryin'. By and by the rain stopped. I went over to the river's edge ever' few minutes to see if anybody washed up, but there wasn't nobody, it weren't no use to hope there would be. All them people must've been drowned or else still on the boat. She was all broke up, halfway out in the river. I don't know how me and Mary-Jane swum it, and I still don't. I knowed we had to get warmed up and dry, or we'd both get pneumonia, so I found all the dry brush I could, and pretty soon we had a good little fire going. I always remembered to carry waterproof matches, that was something Tom Sawyer taught me, even when I wasn't near the water, and I was glad of 'em then.

Well, Mary-Jane, she looked almost happy, sitting there by that fire, even though she was crying and we was both sad about all our friends on the boat who we knew we'd never see again. It wasn't cold once the rain stopped, and we was in a sheltered place so even though the wind was howling still, we was comfortable, or as comfortable as you can be when you've just seen ol' death lookin' you in the eye. Suddenly I said to Mary-Jane, "I wish we could just stay like this and you didn't have to go to England and get married," and she said, "so do I." Then after a minute she said, "Why don't you marry me, Huck?" And damned if I didn't say, "I will, too."

Well, that's how it happened and I wasn't never sorry it did. When we got found the next day, we had it all planned. By the time we got to St. Petersburg, we knowed what we was going to tell the folks.

Aunt Polly and Tom Sawyer and Sid and Mary and Jim and the Widow Douglas, and everyone was there to meet us. They all said it was a miracle, and we was the only ones that had been saved from that wreck. After awhile when everyone had finished talking about how it was a miracle and we'd all had a good feed at Aunt Polly's, and I explained who Mary-Jane was, I told them, right out, Me and Mary-Jane is getting' married!"

Tom Sawyer looked at me like his eyes was going to pop out of his head, and the old folks said a lot of stuff about how we was both in shock from our ordeal, and things like that, but the Widow, she looked at me real hard, and she said, "Huck's a grown-up man now, and I think he knows what he's doing." I could've kissed the old lady for that, and after she said that, everyone else sort of calmed down. The thing was, I <u>was</u> a grown man. I never had no proper childhood, living with Pap, then living on my own like a mongrel dog for so long, and even though I'd been at Aunt Sally's, and I'd had a home, I didn't feel like no child, not at all. And Mary-Jane, well, no one could find no fault with her. And it wasn't like lots of fellas my age didn't get married. Joe Harper, he'd a got married the summer before to Amy Lawrence and they already had a little boy.

So by and by the folks got used to the idea, but Tom Sawyer, he still looked pretty green. After supper we went outside and was having a smoke and Tom, he said, "You serious about this? This marriage, I mean."

He said "marriage" like it give him a stomach ache to say it, and I said, "Yes, I reckon I am."

I looked over at Tom. He was smoking, and he thought himself quite a fella, but I seed he was still a squirt. I was at least a head taller than him, and he still looked like a boy. He looked at me sort of disgusted and said, " When I heard you were coming back, I thought we might have some adventures."

Well, that was just like Tom Sawyer. Seventeen years old and still playing cowboys and robbers. I guess he'd just had it too easy. He never had to have troubles, but he made them for himself to make up for it. I guess I was just different. And when I thought about Mary-Jane crying on the boat, and her pretty face, and how happy she was when I said I'd marry her and she didn't need to go to England, I knew I was doing the right thing. So it was all decided. But Tom, he just couldn't get real happy about it. Aunt Sally and Uncle Silas was wrote to and by the time they wrote back saying it was alright with them, them having met Mary-Jane and knowing that we was old friends anyways, it was all done. Mary-Jane didn't have to answer to no one, being the oldest in the family, and she told her sisters we'd come back and run the farm, and that was just fine with me. And I still had my money in the bank from me and Tom Sawyer's robber days when we found that treasure, so as soon as Aunt Sally arrived, we done it.

Well, I never felt no happier in my life before, nor after, and I know I never will find nothing in life no better than the time me and Mary-Jane was together. We went back to Arkansas and set up on the farm, and we was just like a pair of cooing doves. I still went fishing from time to time, and I still thought about having adventures, but mainly I was content. Mary-Jane, she was as happy as a child. We'd sit up evenings after supper talking and talking, and even though she was so smart, Mary-Jane never found no fault with me. And then after we'd set up a spell, we'd go to bed, and I couldn't write nothing about <u>them</u> times, they was so good they was holy. After a couple of years, I had the farm running good, and everyone said how amazing it was, a rambler like me turning into such a steady man. I was near twenty then, and Mary-Jane, she was about twenty-five. And then it all went wrong, terrible wrong.

Mary-Jane, she was expecting a child. I was as proud as I could be. I'd growed a beard and most people thought I was about twenty-five or so, and I did feel like a respectable man. I was working on the farm, and we had a couple of field niggers, and with that money I had, we'd built ourselves another house and left the old family house to the other two girls. The younger one, she was a-getting married soon, and the older one was already married. She'd had some bad luck though. She had a baby boy, and the poor mite died ten days after it was born. When Mary-Jane found out she was expecting, she didn't want to tell Susan, but in the end she did. Susan was just as happy as she could be for her though. I knowed she would be. All three of them Wilks girls had a lot of sand.

Then the time came for the baby to be born. I had a fair idea of what was coming, but I didn't know how terrible it was going to be. The women, they just sent me out, and I sat on the porch smoking my pipe and thinking about how if the baby was a boy how I'd teach him to fish and hunt, and the high times we'd have together. But after awhile I got up and walked down to the fields. It was taking so long. I could hear Mary-Jane screaming and calling out even from way down in the pasture. I ran back up to the house, but them women wouldn't even let me in the house. I just couldn't stand it and I don't think no man could. There's nothing a man ever goes through like that, and anyone who ever thinks men have got more sand than women ought to try having himself a baby. Well, after what seemed like days, it was over. Susan, she came down and found me, and she said, "Huck, you've got a daughter." I felt happy, but there weren't no happiness in Susan's face. Then she said, "But Mary-Jane's died." Then we both fell to weeping and I just lay on the ground and howled. After awhile I got up and went to the river. Susan looked at me for a long time then went back up to the house to see about the baby. I was a-going to kill myself, I didn't know what else to do. I thought about Mary-Jane's pretty face, and those screams kept echoing in my head. I couldn't take no more. But when I throwed myself in, I just swum, like by instinct. My arms wouldn't let me go under. Ever' time I swallowed some of that muddy water, I come up spitting. I couldn't do it. I don't know how long or how far I swum, or was dragged by the current, but finally, when I was about near dead, I pulled myself up on the bank and I passed out.

When they finally found me, I think I was near dead of cold. I told 'em to just leave me be and let me die, but they took me back up to the house and put me to bed, but I just tossed and turned and kept thinking Mary-Jane was there beside me. I was bad for four or five days, and by the time I come to, Mary-Jane was already six feet under, and I hadn't even seen my child. Susan and Joanna, the other sister, they brought the baby in for me to see, and then Susan she said, "What do you want to call her, Huck?" It was then that I looked at that baby. She was quiet, and pretty for a baby, and she opened her eyes and I kind of touched her face. I don't know why, but I said, "Ruth," it just kind of sprung into my head, and Ruth she was.

Susan and Joanna, they doted on that child, and they seemed to get over Mary-Jane by loving her little girl. And pretty soon Susan was expecting again herself, and I thought, "That child is going to have a mighty nice life in this family," and I knowed it was true.

All the time since Mary-Jane had died and I'd got better, I just worked. If there wasn't nothing to do on the farm, I'd saw logs. And if there weren't no logs to saw, I'd cut down a tree so's I could chop it up. But it weren't no good. One evening, early spring, when I'd been working like a nigger all day, I walked over to the house and I saw Susan sitting on the porch with Ruthie on her lap. She was singing to her, and it brought tears to my eyes, thinking how proud and happy I'd be if her mother was sitting there with her, and how happy Mary-Jane would have been to have had such a beautiful child. I'd been thinking for a few days, and my mind was made up. "Susan," I said, "you sure love that child." And Susan, she looked at me kind of funny, and said, "Of course I do, how could I not?"

And I said, "Do you reckon it'll make any difference when you have one of your own?"

"Oh, no," she said, looking down at Ruth with her eyes just filled with love, "she's like my own."

"Well," I said, swallowing hard, "she is your own now. I give her to you. And the house too, and the farm. I can't stay no more. I know you'll raise her right. You just tell her her Pa couldn't stay around no more. Make sure you tell her that it ain't that I didn't love her, but I just couldn't stay."

They all tried to persuade me not to go, but the next day I went. I'd heard there was gold in California, and even though I didn't need no money, I thought I'd go West. I just had to. I felt like a ghost there, and I think the family, they was probably pretty relieved when I did go, taking my misery with me. I couldn't stay no more in a place where I'd been so happy.

I went down to see Aunt Sally and Uncle Silas and the family before I set off, and I promised to write, though like I said, I wasn't no hand at letter writing, and I think they understood why I had to light out. I was born wild, and even though I'd liked it being tamed, I was going wild again with all my sorrow. That's all most wildness is anyhow, sorrow dressed up diff'rent. There wasn't no way to stop it.

Chapter Two

Pretty soon I was on my way to California. I thought I'd stop and see Tom Sawyer and all them up in St. Petersburg. The Widow, she'd done died a year before, but Tom was still hanging around. Sid and Susie Harper had got married a couple of years before, and they had a little boy about the same age as my little Ruth. I felt sort of strange looking at them two with their little child. It made me go all dark inside, and I walked away. Tom, he come running after me, but Tom, he was still just like a child, he didn't have no real understanding of how a man feels.

Tom was working for Judge Thatcher, training himself to be a lawyer, but he didn't have no real interest in it. Old Judge Thatcher, he'd got Tom a place at West Point, like he'd always said he would, and Tom had gone off there to become a soldier. But it warn't no good. Tom didn't have the grit nor the meanness nohow. When I saw him he'd been back in St. Petersburg more'n a year. But he warn't happy, nor settled. When he heard I was setting off for California, he was so excited he couldn't hardly speak. When he did talk, it was all garbled together, gold and silver and Indians and train robbers and I don't know what all. It's like I said. Tom ain't never growed up, and men like him, they never will. What's kind of sad about it that it's sort of like looking at a ghost. There warn't no better boy than Tom Sawyer could ever be. He was the most perfect one for any kind of good time and adventures when we was boys. He was the respectable one, and me, I was just the grubby orphan with the town drunk for a father, but it didn't make no difference to Tom Sawyer. He was a real democrat, I have to say. But as a man, Tom was different. He still wanted to have that kind of high old time we'd had when we didn't have a care in the world. But me, I'd had cares. Tom never let himself have none, and it was all still a big game to him. But it didn't seem like he was having much fun, he just liked to think he was.

Well, you can see the rest of this train from round the bend. Tom, he quit his lawyering and he sold his horse and before I knew it, we was catching the Nevada stage from St. Jo one rainy morning. We'd got there the day before and had spent the afternoon buying our outfits. I'd got me some good new boots and a couple of pairs of pants and shirts, a couple of blankets and a new hat. That was about all. I figured we'd buy our mining gear once we reached California. But Tom, you'd think he was going to a fancy dress party. He'd done bought himself a real slick new suit and a couple of nice white shirts. He found a hat that made him look like he was fixing to rob a train, all black with a silver band round the crown. He'd got himself some shiny black boots, and he'd bought himself a gun. A great big colt revolver with a big leather holster.

I myself never found no need to carry a gun, at least not when I was a farmer. And I figure if I'm going to be pulling a gun on someone, he's probably going to have pulled his on me faster, so what's the use? And if we get surrounded by a thousand redskins, well what good is six bullets going to do? But Tom, he had to have that gun. My, he thought he was fine. But it didn't bother me too much. It was kind of like watching a child at play. Leastaways that's what I thought.

It cheered me up being with Tom Sawyer again, and after awhile I could even smile without being asked to. It's good to get away after terrible troubles like I'd had. The thing was, before, when I was just a runny-nosed boy that nobody cared about, things might of happened to me that wouldn't of bothered me at all. But having left that sort of world behind when I became a Phelps and then got married to Mary-Jane, it was like all the protection I might a had was gone. It makes you weak, loving people. You ain't never no more vulnerable than when you got your heart full.

It was quite a trip out west in those days, before the trains come through, and stagin' was a rough business. Sometimes we'd ride on the top of the stage, which was best, and sometimes inside. Every six hours or so the stage'd stop at some low down little place where we could get some piece of pitiful animal that had died of sickness or been put out of its misery, which was called steak; and some road sweepin's mixed up with water out'n a dirty bucket which was called coffee. Sometimes there'd be sawdust mixed up with them same road sweepins and baked, which was called bread. But even so, it was quite a ride. I never seen country so grand and empty as them places we saw on our way to California. We rattled on through Kansas and Nebraska country and got to the Great Salt Lake in twelve days from St. Jo. We passed a couple of immigrant trains on our way out. Poor Mormon folks on their way to Zion, they called it, chased out of near ever' where else they went. I couldn't see how they was doin' much harm, but no one seemed to want 'em. You'd see one man with a long beard, and two or maybe three wives in the wagon, and a passel of children. Sometimes we'd see 'em just pullin' handcarts along behind 'em. They must a sure believed in somethin' to go through that. And Salt Lake City, it just looked like a mirage in the desert in those days. It was some pretty lonesome and unfriendly country. And the redskins still a mite lively, too. From Salt Lake it was just a hop, skip and a jump to the goldfields up in the Sierras. It'd just been a few years since them poor lost emigrants had got lost in the mountains and ended up eatin' each other. But now the ways was marked, and people just floodin' in. We landed up near the Comstock about two weeks after we'd seen the Salt Lake.

Tom and me got settled in and commenced prospecting. That country up there it's sure something. There was the deepest, darkest woods, and the prettiest little mountain meadows, and waterfalls, and up higher, glaciers, and I don't know what all. But most of the gold-diggers, they just kept their eyes on the ground. Tom, he did too. I'd go walkin' sometimes when we weren't minin', and I seen some places that were so still and quiet and beautiful that it seemed like God had just finished makin' them. It comforted me some, bein' in those places, almost like I was back with Mary-Jane. But then sometimes you'd hear some old miner shouting and swearin' and all the magic kind of disappeared.

We was at it about eight months, mainly placer mining, and when that wasn't no good we went to work for some diggings up on the Comstock. But Tom, he didn't like working for no one else, no how, and truth to tell, he wasn't much good at the hard work that mining is. Me, I didn't mind. It wasn't much more work than farming. Anyway, one day, Tom comes into the shack we was sharing, looking mighty fed up. He sets down on the old chair that was the only one in the place and says, "Huck, I got to get out of this mining business."

"What you got in mind to do instead?" I asked him.
"Let's go down to San Francisco and see what turns up."
"Alright by me."
Like I said before, I didn't much mind what I was doing, so long as I was busy and didn't have too much time to think about Mary-Jane and how much I still missed her. The mining hadn't come to much anyway. We'd made some money and lost it again, but them miners was a rough old lot and the work was hard. Tom, he thought we'd just get rich quick, like when we found that treasure in Injun Joe's cave, but it warn't like that, leastaways not for us.

So we went down to Frisco. The ride down through the mountains, it was pretty, but when we got down to the where the river runs into the bay, my, it was something to see. Those hills looking out to the Pacific Ocean, and those little islands in the middle of the bay, then the town with those hills going all up and down, it was a sight to see. Tom, he never paid too much attention to the landscape, being more interested in working out deals and such, but as we was crossing over in the ferry I kept thinking, "These hills and places been here since before the bible, before even anybody thought about such things." I reckon I said something of the kind to Tom cause he just kind of looked at me funny then turned to talk to some man he had met on the boat.

Well, when we got into the town, it was a real jamboree. The gold rush had turned San Francisco from a little port into a boom-town in less than two years. And California had just become a state, so there was flags flying ever' where, and people just rushing around. There was lots of miners, like us, too, some of 'em looked pretty down on their luck. I give a dime to more'n one of 'em, but Tom, he says, "We might be needin' it more than them before we're through." And I have to say, I was kind of disappointed in Tom Sawyer then, and I never been so before. I just says to him, "We ain't needin' it now Tom," and I continued whenever I see some old boy asking for a dime to give it to him. Tom he looked kind of disgusted, but I didn't pay him no mind after that.

Well, after we'd walked around through them streets and crowds for awhile, we figured we'd better find us a place to stay, so Tom he goes off one way and I sat down out of the way of the crowds and kept an eye on our things. Well I wasn't sittin, there, just kind of watchin' what was going on, for more'n a minute or two when I felt someone eyeing me. You know what I mean. I looked around but I didn't see no one except one old boy in a kind of tatty coat that looked like it had been nice about fifty years before, and one of them women, which San Francisco was full of in them days. I figured it was her eyeing me, so I just pulled my hat down over my eyes and looked like I was sleepin'. Well, by and by I sensed someone coming over, so I looked up, thinking of our things and not wanting them to get hooked by anyone. I looked up and the old boy, he was looking down at me. He looked kind a familiar, in a sort of nasty way, like an old dog that's bit you once. He keeps looking at me and finally I says, "Do you want something?"

Then it started working on me, and pretty soon I knowed exactly who this old fella was. If you read my other book you'll remember them rascals, the King and the Duke, who tried to rob Mary-Jane's family, like I said at the beginning. Well, standing before me like a sure-nough living ghost was the King himself. Last time I'd seen him he was covered in tar and feathers and sitting a mite uncomfortable on a rail.

Well, you can imagine how I felt. I had married Mary-Jane, and I loved that family, and here was the old no-good that would a left them all three poor as church mice. So I said, "I don't want nothing to do with you."

He kind of huffed around a minute and said a few things about how I'd abandoned him and the Duke, and similar nonsense till I was pretty sick of the sound of his voice. I'd a been sitting down, and then I got up. I think I told you I had grown up to be a big man, over six feet tall, and pretty broad too. Well the King, he warn't no more'n about five-feet-five, and he looked a little sick when he sees me get up, so he changed his tune. He starts going on how good it was to see me, and what a fine feller I'd become, and what happened to my old nigger Jim, what <u>he</u> and that other fraud, the Duke, had tried to return to slavery for forty dollars. Well, I says again, I didn't want nothing to do with him, and I would a walked away, except I knew Tom Sawyer would be coming back to find me there, and I didn't know how we'd locate each other if I left where he thought I'd be waitin.

Well, he was going on enough to make a man sick, like he was my old uncle or something, so I leaned over toward him, and said, "Go away. I didn't like you then and I don't like you now and I don't want none of you."

Well then he changes his tune again and says how he's fallen onto hard times and hasn't had nothing to eat for three days and could I help a fellow southerner out for old times' sake.

I knew he'd just spend it on whiskey, but I gave him a dollar. I told him to get away from me and not come back or I'd take that dollar out of his hide. Well, he shot away like he'd seen a rattle snake once he got that dollar, and about that time, Tom Sawyer he come back.

Tom saw the King scuttling away and he kind of looked at him then says to me, "Who's that?"

Well, I'd told him the stories of my trip down the river with Jim on the raft, and as soon as I reminded him, he remembered the story. Well, it looked to me like ever' bit of old river trash was making its way west, and I says so to Tom.

"What's that make us then?" he says. "We ain't river trash."

"Well, if we ain't, what are we? It looks to me like ever' single person in the United States that hasn't got no reason to be where they are is just flooding into this here gold rush to try to give themselves a reason to be somewhere."

I guess I sounded kind of bitter, after what had happened to me and all, but I didn't mean to upset Tom. I kept forgettin' that to him it was all still an adventure, or he liked to think it was. The trouble with still thinkin' like a boy when you've got to be a man is that you're bound to be disappointed in pret' near everything. Nothing has that kind of magic it used to, and if you don't find some kind of magic in the grown-up world, like I had done with Mary-Jane, you're forever looking for what used to make you feel happy. Even though I had lost Mary-Jane, I <u>knew</u> what grown-up happiness was like, and it comforted me some. Tom, he never had that, and the way he was goin' I didn't think he ever would. So he was always looking for that thing you feel when you're a boy and you've just played hooky after lunch and not been caught, and you get to the river and it's a sunny bright day, and no one around, and then you see a line you left in the water the day before has got a nice fresh fish on it, and you go for a swim, and make a little fire and cook your fish, and lay by the river in the sunshine and quiet and have a smoke, well, it's pretty nice. But that kind of thing, you remember it, but you can't do it again. That was the trouble with Tom, he thought you could keep it up and have it all feel the same. All that happens then is that even what you remember gets all clouded up with disappointment. I felt sorry for Tom that he'd never learned that yet, and I was sorry to sound so bitter around him. It was like sounding bitter around a child. They don't understand it and it just hurts them.

Well, Tom, he was quiet a minute, then he says, "I found us a place." So we humped up our gear and headed out to where Tom had got us a room. There was a lot of building going on and you could just smell raw timber everywhere. This place where Tom had found us a room was on the very end of a street somewhere not far from the harbor. You could see all the way out to the Pacific Ocean, and I liked it just fine. I reckon by now there's hardly a house in San Francisco that can see the ocean, cept'n those that are the very last ones before the waves come crashing in. But in those days it was different. The lady that owned that house was a Mexican and she didn't speak much English. There was about ten fellers bunkin down in her place. She cooked dinner and gave us a bed for a dollar a day each. Tom thought we'd done pretty well finding anywhere at all to stay, the town was so full of miners and fellers that wanted to be miners, and miners going back home, and Mexicans, and sailors coming from the Pacific or round the Horn, and Chinamen, and Islanders and whatever other kind of people you choose to name. Why in our house alone there was two Eye-talians, an Englishman, four Mexicans that was somehow related to the lady that ran the place, and a Hindoo who'd been on a ship out of Nantucket and jumped ship in Frisco to go to the gold fields. Well, he'd been to the gold fields and now he wanted to get back home. It was like the whole world had come to California to get rich.

We stayed in that house most a month, lookin' around during the day for something Tom thought was "suitable" for us adventurers, as he liked to call us. Most evenings we'd go out to the saloons. I never was much a hand at drinkin'. Havin' been brought up by Pap kinda put me off it, but Tom, he'd developed quite a taste for whiskey. One evening, Tom and me decided to take a stroll down to the beach. It wasn't very far and the night was fine. We got down there and sat down on the sand in the moonlight and had a smoke. You could see them breakers rolling in, all white and shimmery in the moonlight. And I was thinking to myself, this ocean don't stop till it hits China. And it made me feel kind of funny and happy at the same time thinking about all that space of water and how it had always been there and no one even knowed about China till Columbus discovered America. And then I got to looking at the stars and thinking how far away <u>they</u> were, and wondering if there was anyone sittin on one of them stars lookin out at their sky and wonderin if someone was lookin back at them. Well, it does make you feel small, that kind of thinkin, but not small like a bug that's going to get squashed by the next big foot that comes along, but small like a drop of water in the ocean, or a grain of sand on the beach, small, but part of it all, if you know what I mean.

I didn't say nothin to Tom about what I was thinking, cause I could tell he was figuring something out, and I was right. After a while he jumps up and says, "Tarnation, Huck, what're we doing just sitting here? Let's go into town and see what's up."

Well, I was contented being where I was, but Tom obviously warn't, so off we went. After a spell we found ourselves in a saloon, just crawlin' with folks, men, miners, and women, you know, the kind of women that spends their time in those places. Tom, he had a few drinks and got to bein' friendly with one of 'em, and before I knew it, off he goes with her.

Well, even though I had such a rough upbringin', with Pap and all, I guess I got saved before I could get too corrupted, and then gettin' married so young I never did have no call to go skirt-chasin' too much. But Tom he was different. He kept fallin' in love all the time when he was a boy, but as a man he didn't seem to have much luck with women. I sure didn't think no Frisco fancy woman was the place to start, but Tom, he always did what he wanted and couldn't no one tell him otherwise.

I would a gone back to our house, but I thought I'd better wait for Tom, so I was sittin' there, proppin' up the bar, when suddenly I had somethin' else to think about.

The saloon doors swung open and in walks a feller, all dressed in black, with a black string tie and a white shirt, and a long black cape lined in some shiny red stuff, with a woman looked most like a painted doll on his arm, and a couple of other rough lookin' fellers accompanyin' 'em.

"That's the proprietor," the barman says, kind of winkin' as he speaks, and I didn't think no more about it but turned back to the bar, but I could still see him and his floozy through the mirror glass.

Suddenly I heard a shout and a commotion, and damned if it wasn't that rascal I'd seen the day we arrived, the King, a running up to this proprietor. People quieted down a bit to have a look at the fuss and I could hear what the old idiot was saying.

"Bilgewater, is it really you? After all these years, I can't believe it! Thank God I've found you! I've fallen on to hard times and now like a miracle I find my old companion of the river!" He went on like this for a good while, and said a lot more sniveling kind of stuff, but I just put my head down and hoped they wouldn't see me. It was the Duke alright, and here was the King probably tellin' him he'd found me too. I felt sick, I can tell you.

Well the Duke, after a minute or two he recognizes the King, and he claps his arm around him and brings him up to the bar for a drink. They opened a bottle and started drinkin' and jawin' about one thing and another. Why the two old frauds actually looked like they was glad to se each other.

I was just fixin' to sort of siddle out without them seeing me when out from some room comes Tom Sawyer and <u>he</u> sings out, "Huck! Where you goin'?"

Well the King and the Duke turns and looks at me, and the King tells the Duke how he'd seen me before, and the Duke he gets a big smile on his face like a snake about to bite someone and comes over. Tom, he'd come back by now, and I told him who the Duke was, and the Duke says why don't we come on over and have a drink, no hard feelings, old times' sake and all that.

I didn't want to celebrate no old times with those two scallywags, but Tom, he says, "Come on, what's the harm?"

So we joined 'em and sat down and talked a little about the river and the Nonesuch and it <u>was</u> kind of funny to think about it all again. After while the Duke says, "You can see those days are long behind me," kind of lookin' around proud.

"How'd you get this here set-up?" I asked him. It turns out that the Duke had come out early when the gold strike hit, and he was one of the lucky ones. He got a strike up on Sutter Creek after pret' near everyone else had moved on, and he'd struck big. He sold his claim out and high-tailed it down to Frisco with the cash. Turns out his claim was salted, but that didn't matter to him none, he had the money.

"It wasn't me that salted that mine," he says, all oily and smiling. "That claim had been worked by an old boy for a year or more. He fell off a ridge one day and his claim come up and I bought it. The old rascal must have salted it just before he went to his reward."

"Makes you think, don't it?" I said.

He didn't say nothin' to that but just went on. Seems as how a syndicate bought him out and mined it for a few months and come up with nothin' more than the few saltins'. He looked around kind of nervous when he said that. I reckoned someone was after him now, but I didn't say nothin'.

One thing led to another, and before I could stop him, Tom Sawyer had told the Duke how we was lookin' for something to do, and was wondering maybe if he had some ideas. I could a told Tom Sawyer that man wouldn't put no one on to no good thing, but Tom was all full of plans and ideas, and it looked to him like the Duke was too. Well the Duke, he smiled, all oily like, and he turned to one of his rough boys who was a hangin' round him all the time and says, "What about the cargo business? I think these fellers would be likely for that." The rough guy just sort of grunted and says, "Whatever you think, boss." Then the Duke he turns to us.

"The thing is fellers, I got some business down at the harbor. There's a ship there headin' out in the morning for the Sandwiches then down to Australia. If you go down there and tell the man on the deck that I've sent you - say Roberts has sent you - and that you're there about the cargo. He'll sort you out. Then come see me tomorrow morning."

Well Tom, he was up like a shot. He didn't even wait to see what the business was a goin' to be. He just asked the name of the ship and out we went. Well, I was suspicious from the start, but Tom he just said I was full of foolishness, that obviously the Duke was a successful man and wouldn't have no call to be nothin' but generous to us, and more along that line. I didn't want no argument with Tom, but I thought to myself that success don't make someone bad, good. It just makes them able to look the part. And what kind of success that old rascal had had was on the backs of other people, I'd be bound. But that ain't the way most people think.

Well, we got down to the ship, which was called the Flying Dutchman, and we went up to the side and yelled. The ship was a mite run down lookin', loomin' up out of the water, all dark, with the moonlight behind. It give me the shivers. After a minute or two some beat-up looking feller show up at the side of the ship. "What you want?" he says, as unpleasant as you like.

"Roberts sent us," Tom says, "about the cargo."

Well, the feller on the boat kind of snorts and goes away. We heard him a-talkin' to someone in low voices. Then another feller, a little more likely looking than the other comes up and says, "Come up on board."

The rough boy, he put down an old rickety gangway, and me and Tom filed up onto that old hulk. I knowed I was doin' something stupid, but I still didn't much care if I was live or dead, so on I went. Tom just acted like he was goin' on a Sunday picnic.

"Cargo's in here," the rough boy said, leading me and Tom toward the hold. "Go on down there and you'll find two cases, you just grab 'em and take 'em back to Roberts."

I was just about to say something about how he didn't want it till the morning and I think I had just opened my mouth when suddenly I seen stars, and they weren't the ones in the sky, and then ever' thing went dark.

Well, the next time I opened my eyes I didn't know if it were day or night. My head hurt powerfully and I felt pretty sick. My hands was tied too, and I felt like I was in a barrel goin' over Niagra Falls, I was pitchin' and rollin' so much. I heard a groan nearby, and in the dark I made out Tom. "Tom," I says, "you alright Tom?" Tom he grunted somethin' and then he was sick. After a minute he sat up. His hands was tied too, but our feet was free.

"We're prisoners," I said. "I guess the cargo was us. I should a known that rogue wouldn't wish us no good."

"You did know, Huck," says Tom, "but I didn't listen. I'm sorry."

Well, that's the first time I ever heard Tom Sawyer say he was sorry for anything, and I thought, maybe he's becomin' a man after all. About then, there was a noise and the hatch above us opened and the daylight streamed in on us like a couple of gophers turned up by a spade.

"Gimme your hands," someone says, and reaches down and cuts the cords tying us up, "and get long up here."

We got up on deck and way far away we could see the coast. "That's Californy," the man who'd cut our ropes said. "You won't be seeing her for a spell."

"You've kidnapped us," Tom started out, and was about to say something else when the captain cracked him across the mouth. Tom looked shocked, then mean. There was a little line of blood drippin' out of the corner of his mouth.

"You haven't been kidnapped, you been impressed on board this ship. Your friend Roberts owed me money and said he'd provide me with two sailors to repay the debt, and you are them. You'll sail with us to Australia and then you can get off and live among the convicts, I don't care. Or you can sign on then as free sailors and come back with us. Take your choice. I'm no pirate, but I know when I'm owed."

"But we ain't his friends," I said, "he tricked us."

"That doesn't make any difference to me. I was owed two sailors and I got them. Now get some food and then get to work."

Well, I reckoned the captain knew he was doin' wrong, or he wouldn't have knocked us out before we had a chance to say anything, but except for that, I could see his point. And after while, it weren't no bad life, being on that ship. He wasn't a pirate, that was sure, but he was a hard man. There was about twenty-five of us, but Tom and me was the only hijacked ones. Ever' other man there had signed on free. Some were miners that had got fed up with the goldfields. Some was sailors out of Nantucket and Boston whose ships was abandoned by the sailors gettin' gold fever. Some was Mexicans. There was a couple of Chinamen and a nigger from Alabama. Tom and me figured he was a runaway, but we wasn't going to say anything, havin' had something to do with runaway niggers ourselves and not bein' in any position to criticize.

After we left San Francisco, we went down the coast a ways to Los Angeles. The captain said he'd tie me and Tom up if we looked like trying to jump ship, but we said we wouldn't. There wasn't nothin' there but a little village and some Mexicans, and then there was the desert behind that. I figured we was better off on the ship than out there. He took on some cargo, and then we was out to the open sea.

After I got my sea legs and stopped feeling sick all the time, I felt like if I saw the Duke again, I'd shake his hand. There ain't no life like the sea. All the time when I was a boy and thinkin' how I'd light out for the territories, I just thought about how it was all out there, that empty land, and all the adventures I'd have in it. But when it come to it, and Tom and me made our way to California, it was like it was all past and over. I mean, we hadn't seen all the wild country, but we'd got through it and we were at the end. Now we were goin' even further west, west of west, if you see what I mean.

And the sea, there ain't nothin' like it. Sometimes of an evening I'd sit up at the front of the boat and look out. The stars would be shinin' and sometimes a little cloud would scud across the moon. I'd sit there and think about things, and even though I'd lost what mattered to me most when Mary-Jane died, I felt sort of comforted, almost like she was there with me, out there in all that emptiness, I didn't never feel alone.

Tom, he was different. He sulked quite a lot at first, and he didn't like the work. Sailoring is as hard as farming, I'd say. Tom liked adventures, but plain hard work had always missed him somehow. But he got by. After a few weeks he'd made a few friends among the crew, and he was pretty good at getting people to do things for him. He always was like that. What bothered him most, I'd say, was the idea that he was wastin' time. Tom had it figured that ever' thing in the world that was worth happening was in California, and to feel like he was missin' the show pained him. But he settled down after awhile. He played cards a lot with the crew, and growed a beard, so that by the time we got near Hawaii, the Sandwich Islands they're called, we both looked pret' much like old tars.

The Captain wasn't worried about us jumpin' ship no more, and as for me, I couldn't imagine any life that suited me better. I just figured I'd stay a sailor for the rest of my life. So when we got to Hawaii and docked in Honolulu harbor, me and Tom was let off with the rest of the sailors to have a look around.

It's quite a sight when you been at sea, two, nearly three weeks, and not seen so much as a rowboat or a rock, to see them islands. First you see a little tip of somethin'. Then, as you're sailin', a little more appears. Pretty soon you can see the whole island, just shinin' in the sunlight, and then you can smell it too. The first smell of Hawaii is somethin' I don't think anyone ever forgets. Like perfumes, just waftin' over the sea, all fruit and flowers and sea and sand mixed up in it. It kind of knocks you over.

Well, I never seen such a place. The town was pretty, all painted white and lots of different little houses, and the trees and flowers all over the place. Why, I ate kinds of fruit I never knew grew on the earth. And the mountain up above. Why, it was just like paradise. And the people! The Hawaiians, Kanakas they call themselves, were about the prettiest people I ever seen. They were nearly black, but not like niggers, sort of dark brown from the sun. The fellers were mostly big and good looking, but the gals! I never seen such women. They walked around with hardly anything on most of the time, it was so hot, and beautiful! Long black hair and fine eyes. And you should see them when they swim, just like fishes. I couldn't keep from looking at them, even though I did feel like I shouldn't, on account of Mary-Jane. But Tom, he wasn't that interested. He looked around and looked up towards the mountain they call Di'mond Head, and said, "I wonder if there's real di'monds up there?" I said I didn't know and didn't care. I said I'd rather stay on the beach eating poi and mangoes with the girls than go hunting for a shipload of di'monds. We went back to the ship that night and the Captain said we'd be a week picking up cargo and takin' on stores and water, then we'd head off to Tahiti.   A few days later, I went off into the island by myself. It was hot, but I'd been in Louisiana in the summertime, so it was just like a spring day. I walked up as far as I could go into those hills and up towards Di'mond Head. It was noisy country, full of birds screechin' and little animals runnin' underfoot. Water ever' where, runnin' out of the mountain. I came upon a waterfall with a pool underneath, and I was that hot that I just took off my clothes and dived right in. I don't think I've ever known anythin' better than swimmin' in that cool water with that waterfall splashin' down and the green ever' where. Kind of like Adam and Eve in paradise, but warn't no Eve, I remembered, then I got to feelin' low again and went back down to the ship.

That night Tom comes and finds me on my watch. "Huck," he says, whispering, "I ain't going to Tahiti."

"What're you going to do then?"

"I'm going to jump ship the night before we leave and catch the next ship back to Frisco. You coming?"

Well, I thought long and hard about what Tom was proposing. I'd always let him lead me into trouble, but usually it ended up alright. This time I wasn't so sure. Even if we had been kidnapped, we were sailors on the Flying Dutchman now, and no one was going to believe us over the Captain. And anyway, I liked sailoring, and I liked these islands. I had a yen to see Tahiti, and to look at Australia, where no one lives except wild savages and English murderers. So I did something Tom hadn't expected. I told him no.

Tom looked stunned, and then perplexed, and then after that he looked a little mad. He walked off leavin' me there on the deck. I didn't mind though, even though we'd always been such good friends, nohow.

Chapter Three

By the time it was noticed that Tom wasn't on board, we were heading west out of Honolulu with a brisk wind behind us. There wasn't no way the Captain was turnin' back for one sailor, and truth to tell, no one much missed Tom. He hadn't pulled his weight and all his schemes seemed like foolishness once he wasn't around to tell them himself. I missed him at first, but then I got to liking being on my own. It had been good to have him around, but truth to tell, we was better friends when we was boys. Tom was a great boy, like I said before, but just a tolerable man. Now I was just as happy alone. I guess all the things I had been through had kind of toughened me up. You ain't afraid of your own company once you've looked into that black pit.

We were on a course for Tahiti and we just sung along. We had good winds behind us, and it wasn't too hot, being March, nor too stormy yet, though I did hear that there are some howlers out there in the springtime. Truth to tell, there wasn't too much to do on the ship once we was underway. She was in good trim by then, and we wasn't whalin', so we kept her up and kept her clean, but a lot of the time we had to ourselves.

I used to go up to the top of the mainmast sometimes and just look out. Up there, you can see that the earth is a ball, and that the ship and all of us on it was just specks crawling over that ball. I never been up on no mountaintops, so I don't know if it's the same, but being up there on that mast and lookin' out over all that sea, just surrounding us and going on forever, I felt like I understood what people meant when they talked about God. Not like the Widow's God with a long white beard and a thunderbolt, no somethin' different that I ain't got the words to say. But I know what I mean. Later on in my life, the part I'll tell about later - when I was on the plains, I felt somethin' similar - like I was a part of it all. I never did feel no fear in those places.

One day I was up on the mast, loafin' and looking, when I see a speck on the horizon. It wasn't too common for us to have company out there, so I sung out, "Ship on the starboard!" and ever' body runs to the starboard side to have a look. It was so far off then only I could see it, but by and by it come into view. The Captain he looks through his spyglass for a long time, then he put it down and cursed something terrible. He ordered all sails up and we went singin' along in front of the wind then. In fact, quite a storm was blowin' up, but we kept all the sail up. It was pirates I'd seen, and they was gainin' on us. Luck was with us that day though, that wind she blew into a proper hurricane, most, and we lost her.

What I thought afterwards, was how was it, that in the whole of the ocean, that pirate ship ought to find us. And there we was, on the same stretch of ocean, but a minute either way, and she'd of missed us, and we'd of missed her. If we'd a been lookin' for her, it'd of been a miracle we found each other, as it was, it was almost a disaster. But the next day, we wasn't so lucky.

That storm blowed itself out about three o'clock the next day. We were pretty beat up. A couple of sails had got ripped, and the ship, she looked like a whore who'd been in a cat-fight back in Frisco. But she was still makin' way pretty good. But pretty soon the lookout shouted, "Ship to port!" and damn if that pirates' boat hadn't come up behind us, and caught up a good deal in the storm too. She was bigger'n us, and she had guns. I knew we was in for it. Well pretty soon she drew up alongside. The captain knew it wasn't no good to try to outrun her, and if we fired on her with the few rifles and pistols we had, why she'd a blown us out of the water with those cannons. So we just waited.

She come up alongside and we could see their faces. They were an evil lookin' crew, Malays, mostly, but a few niggers and a couple of Kanakas, or maybe south sea islanders, I couldn't tell. But the captain, he was a white man.

"Where bound?" the pirate captain shouts out to us.
"Tahiti, then Australia, shipmate," our captain calls out.

"What cargo?"

"Provisions for the convict colony."

Now this got me thinkin'. I had been down in the hold more'n once, and I didn't see nothin' that looked like provisions. There was a lot of iron bound boxes though, and once I hit my foot on one and it didn't even move it was so heavy. I figured it was gold we had in there, but I couldn't figure why we was takin' it to Australia, no way.

So when our captain says, "provisions," the other captain just sort of laughed. "Board her!" he shouts to his crew, and they grappled her close and before we knew it we was just swarmin' with pirates. They bought up those boxes, heavin' and groanin' and got 'em onto the other ship. We had to help, and pretty soon our hold was just about empty. Our captain just sat in his chair on the deck and watched with a grim look on his face. When all the cargo was shifted, the pirate captain said, "We're much obliged, Captain. I'm a pirate, but I'm not a murderer, and you and your crew can go along to Tahiti with my compliments." He kind of bowed then and turned away, but our captain says, "How'd you know we had gold?"

The pirate captain turns back and says, "Roberts let me know there was some interesting cargo heading towards the Antipodes."

So the Duke had been in on this one too. He'd certainly come up in the world since his days as a river rat.

The pirate crew got back on their ship and unhooked the grapples and we separated. But when the pirates was about three hundred feet away, they swung their biggest cannon round. We seen what whaps happening and every man jumped for the sails, but it was too late. That ball hit us amidships and we hardly had time to get the boats down before she went, nose first, down to Davy Jones' locker.

Well, I could tell you about them weeks in the long boats, but I don't like to think about them much. I'll just say there was a lot of sufferin' and dying, and a storm knocked the other boat all to bits and most all the sailors drowned, and some of 'em was my friends, and all of 'em was my shipmates. Finally there was just me and the captain left in the one boat. We'd dropped our last shipmate in the sea that morning after he finally gave up the ghost, and it was just horrible to see them sharks tearin' up what was left of him. We'd been adrift near a month. Our water was near gone. The little food there had been was long gone. We'd been living on raw fish and seagulls, but neither of us had much strength left to even try to catch anything. When I looked at the captain, I wondered if I looked as horrible as he did. It was like looking at a skeleton with eyes. But dead as the rest of him looked, his eyes was still livin', almost unnaturally so.

The sun burned down terribly, and we made what shade we could from our rags. I was driftin' into something like sleep when suddenly the captain croaks,

"There isn't enough water for two."

I kind of looked at him and then closed my eyes again, but something made me look up. He was comin' for me, with them wild eyes, with an oar-end above his head. I shifted just in time and grabbed his arm. I'd a never thought someone that near dead would have that kind of fight in him. He was like a tiger. Finally I knocked his head on the side of the gunnel and he went still. I was afraid I'd killed him, but then we was both so near dead it didn't much matter. After a spell, though, he spoke.

"I'm sorry, Huck. I was crazy. Forgive me."

I didn't say nothin', but I turned away and closed my eyes. He could kill me if he wanted. I didn't care no more. But suddenly the boat heaves and I heard a splash. It didn't take long for the sharks to find him. So I was alone.

I had enough water for maybe a day or two more, but no food. I thought maybe I should take the captain's way out, but somethin' stopped me. Maybe it was the thought of Mary-Jane's face, or thinkin' about my little Ruthie at home. I vowed if I got out of that boat alive, I'd go back to Arkansas and see them all again.

The next few days I was barely conscious. One night I fell into a kind of sleep and woke to see the stars shinin'. They wasn't any stars I recognized. There was somethin' different in the air too, a different smell. I put my head up over the gunnel and looked but I couldn't see nothin'. I just put my head back down and closed my eyes. There wasn't no more water and I figured I might as well just go then. I guess I fell asleep cause I felt a jolt and I opened my eyes. Then another, then a sound of scraping like sand. I was really awake then and I looked out. Over the side of the boat I could see land, outlined against the moonlight, and my boat had found its way onto the beach. I got up and drug myself out. My legs hardly worked after sittin' in that boat all them weeks. I dragged through the surf and got up the beach. Then I fell down onto the sand and didn't know no more.

When I woke up the next morning, I wondered if I had died and I was in heaven. But then I felt how thirsty I was and thought maybe this was hell. I staggered along the beach for awhile and finally come upon a stream. I lay there on the sand with my face in that stream till I couldn't drink no more. I never tasted nothin' better. Then I sat up and looked around. I was on an island, but how big I couldn't say. Then I looked out to see and I saw a terrible sight. The longboat was driftin', maybe half a mile out. I knew I didn't have the strength to swim out to her, so I was stranded. I thought of how much Tom Sawyer might have liked the idea of being stranded on a desert island, but he didn't have no idea of what it involved, nohow.

I rambled around that day and found some shell fish and there was fruit on the trees inland. I kept close to that stream though. I didn't feel like I could get enough water. When night was drawin' in I found a kind of sheltered place among the palms above the beach. It wasn't cold.

After a few days, I felt myself getting stronger and I felt like I could risk exploring a little. The only problem was going to be how to carry water. I didn't know if there'd be another stream and I didn't mind gettin' hungry, but I never wanted to be thirsty again. I found a coconut fallen and cracked near the top. I still had my knife with me, so I hollowed it out and filled it with water and sort of sealed up the gap with leaves. It wasn't perfect, but it did. I set off inland. I almost felt like a boy again, settin' off for adventures in the Missouri woods. Tom Sawyer <u>would</u> have liked this part of being shipwrecked, I thought.

I followed the stream for a good way, and I never seen no sign of people. There was plenty of wildlife, birds just ever' where, and little animals scurryin' away whenever I'd get near. Nothin' very big though, and not too many bugs. After awhile the land began to rise and I could see I was on the slopes of a hill or mountain. Pretty soon the trees and bushes kind of slipped away behind me, and I was properly climbin'. The higher I got the more I could see, and ever' thing I saw told me I was on an island. It got cold up there too. A couple of times I passed little streams that were steamin', like the hot springs back home. After a few hours I come right out on a ridge, and above me was the top of the mountain. I knew I had to get there to see what was on the other side, but I didn't want to. She was a volcano alright, and smoke and steam was just pouring from the top.

I knew I had to find out what kind of a place I was in. All I could see from where I was sea and shore, so if it wasn't an island, it was the tip of a peninsula anyway. But what I didn't know was how I was going to get round that volcano to see what was on the other side. I couldn't go no further the way I had come, so I turned around and went back. When I got back down to the beach it was nearly dark and I was worn out, but I seen something that give me back my strength. Out beyond the waves was my boat.

I ran down that beach and jumped in the water and swum out to her. She was further out than I thought, and it took some doing to get her in, but after about an hour there she was, up on the beach, and I knew how I was goin' to get to the other side of the volcano.

I spent a week patchin' her up as best I could. She'd had a sail, but it was all in tatters, but there was still a couple of oars left. For havin' been as rough treated as that boat was, she was still pretty sound and didn't take too much water on.

One morning I filled her up with as much fruit and water as I could, and pushed off. I got her out beyond the breakers and into the clear water. When I was a little way out I seen that where I'd come in was the only place I could of landed without killing myself. That little beach was about the only natural landing place on that side. I rowed for awhile, being careful not to get too far from shore, and then fell into a current. I got round to where I could see the volcano from the east side and kept on going.

Well, it took me two days to circumnavigate that island, but then I knew it was an island, and no other land in sight. I was happy when I got back to my beach. I hadn't seen another landing place anywhere along that coast. So not only was I shipwrecked on an island, I was shipwrecked on half an island, 'cause there was no way I was going to be able to get round that volcano on land.

I got to thinkin' about me an Jim on that island in the Mississippi, and how lonely I felt when I thought I was there by myself, and how happy I was when I found Jim, when he'd run away from Miss Watson. "Tarnation, I'd be glad to see Jim now!" I said aloud, and my own voice sounded strange to me in all that emptiness.

I got used to livin' on the island. By and by I explored nearly all of it that I could get to. It was about ten miles round, but where the volcano was in the middle, it had made a wasteland to the west and east, full of boulders and rocks, and holes in the earth with steam coming out. I went back more than once to see if there was a way across to the other side of the island, but the ground there was too hot to walk on, and there was a drop on one side, so that was out too.

I sailed round again, and finally did find a place where I could land the boat. But that side of the island was full of stinking swamps and not much else. So I went back to my side and stayed.

I found a cave in a cliff face up above the beach. Mainly I stayed down near the stream and the beach, but I was glad to know where that cave was in case trouble looked like coming. I made a rope ladder out of vines and hooked it up there. I'd go up from time to time, and if it rained. I had a good stock of wood there and the rock was so full of little holes I didn't need no chimney. After awhile I got to spending more and more time there, I had made it so comfortable. Up on a point I'd gathered a lot of wood, and I kept a fire burnin' there most all the time, as a signal for any boats might pass.

During the day I'd fish, and sometimes hunt. I made a bow and arrow which worked pretty good. There had been some fish-hooks in the long boat which I still had. Clothes wasn't much of a problem, it was so balmy, but by and by I was about naked, so I set out to find some animals whose skin I could use to make some clothes. I found a big rat kind of animal which wasn't too smart and was pretty easy to catch. It took me about twenty five of them to make me a pair of breeches, but I felt fine when I had done that. Then it took about another fifty to make a shirt. I never knew I was no tailor before.

So that's what I did. There wasn't much point in worrying about life, cause it was enough trouble livin' it. And there was no way I could get off that island less I set off in some direction not knowin' if I was going anywhere at all. So I stayed put.

I used to wonder sometimes what everybody I knew was doing. I wondered if Tom Sawyer had made it back to Frisco, and I wondered if he wondered what had happened to me. I guessed nobody in the world knew if I was alive or dead, and Mary-Jane's sisters probably thought I'd just forgotten about them and my little Ruthie. Sometimes I got to feelin' so sorry for myself I'd sit down on the beach and cry, but mainly I just got on.

I used to talk to myself aloud, just to hear the sound of a human voice, sometimes I'd sing, but it sounded so lonesome and pitiful I couldn't hardly stand it. I guess I had just about become a wild man.

After a couple of years I was walkin' on the beach one day when I spied a sail. I jumped up and down and screamed and shouted and waved. I was going to go and stoke up my fire for a signal when I see the ship was comin' in. I run up to my cave to get a better view, and when I did my heart just about stopped. It was them pirates. I recognized the ship cause it had red wolf carved on the bow. I ain't never forgot that. I run down to the beach and cleared away all signs I'd been there, then I run back up to my cave and pulled up the rope ladder. I was glad that I'd been patchin' up my boat and she was out of sight round beyond the stream where some little trees grew. I could see pretty good without them seeing me. They anchored and then they put down a long boat and rode her into the beach. There was the captain in it, and what looked like some kind of a Kanaka chief, and a woman. There was a couple of Malays rowing, and another islander standin' in the bow with a rifle trained on them two prisoners. I figured I knew what was goin' to happen and I wished I had a gun. But the big Kanaka was talkin' to the captain like he knew him. He kept lookin' at the girl and pointin' and pointin' back to the Captain and shoutin' something. They got to the beach and they all came in. The girl sort of stumbled and one of them Malays pushed her so she fell. I wished I had a gun again, it made me so mad to see him mistreatin' her like that. They all got up to the beach and was havin' some kind of pow-wow. I couldn't hear, but I could tell it warn't too happy a kind of discussion. After awhile it got pretty heated and I could see there was going to be trouble. I knew it was dangerous, but I had a plan. I come out of the cave and up along a ridge above where they were on the beach. At the top of it was the place where I made my signal fires. I figured the brush and wood fallin' would make enough of a distraction. I breathed in and then screamed, as loud as I could, the most war-like sounding screech imaginable, then I pushed that brush off the ridge so that it made a racket like anything. I run back along the ridge and back to my cave where I could see them, and sure enough, all but the islander and the Kanaka girl had run to see what it was. Then I come down the other side with my bow and arrow and when he was lookin' the other way, I shot that islander square in the back. I didn't like to shoot no man in the back, but I knew I had to or it was the girl that would get it. He fell over, and the girl turned, but didn't scream. I signaled to her to come and she understood right away and come runnin' to where I was. I grabbed her hand and run with her back up to the cave. 'Bout that time the others all come runnin' back and when they see the dead islander they stopped stone-still. They looked around a minute, then they all high-tailed it for the boat. I reckon they'd had enough of that place and they figured there was islanders all around. The big Kanaka started shoutin' and pointin' towards where I'd run, but they didn't pay him no mind. I guess I looked savage enough that he didn't think I was no white man anyway. The Kanaka tried to get in the boat, but the captain pushed him away. He swam after the boat, and kept swimming. Finally the captain turned around and took aim with his pistol and shot. There was a little stream of red and then he sunk. We watched them get back to the ship, and then they weighed anchor and sailed out. Pretty soon they was out of sight, but I knew it might be just a trick, so we stayed put. They didn't come back though.

I figured by the time Lani arrived on the island, I'd been there two and a half, three years. It took us a while to understand each other, but finally we did. She had been kidnapped by those pirates. The big Kanaka was in with that crew. When we found his body, all bloated by the sea a few days after the pirates had gone, she just took a rock and smashed the head of it. I couldn't hardly blame her, but it's not the kind of thing you expect to see a woman do.

I told her, as much as I could, what had happened to me. She didn't seem surprised by any of it. I think she was from one of the islands near Tahiti, but I never did make it out exactly.

After all those months and years by myself, I hardly knew how to be around another person. She knew so much more about how to get by on an island than I did. She looked around and found some plants up near the slopes of the volcano that she planted down near the beach. And she knew which roots you could eat, and how to cook those rat animals I'd just used the skins of. I'd tried to eat them before, but I near choked, they were so foul. She knew all that. It was just wonderful having company, and soon we became like man and wife. It was her that did it. I'd a wanted to, but I wasn't goin' to force myself on her, her bein' alone and unprotected with just me. But one night she just come and lay down with me, and that was it.

It wasn't like with Mary-Jane, but it was good. That island which looked like a prison to me before was like a paradise now. We would go swimmin' together and walking, and after a few months we could understand each other pretty good. She shaved me with a sharp shell and cut my hair so I looked like a man and not a wild animal, and she tattooed me. I didn't want to at first, but it seemed to mean so much to her, I let her. She knew how to make the ink from plants that grew there, and she used a sharp bone to do it. I got a back and chest just covered with signs and symbols like nothin' no Christian has ever seen.

After a few months I could see she was expectin' a child, and it worried me, but she just seemed to take it in her stride. When the baby was born, she didn't make a sound except at the end. He was a fine little boy. She called him a Kanaka name, but I called him Tom.

We went along like that for four or five years, and soon I realized I'd been on the island nearly seven years. It must have been 1857 or 58 by then. We had a little girl besides our boy, and she was expecting another when the volcano started to rumble.

The mountain had always smoked and steamed, but this was different. There was rumbling coming from beneath the earth too. One night it got bad. I went out and climbed up to where I could see the cone. Flames was shooting out of it and lava was pouring down the other side from us. We were safe still. But not for long.

About a week later I was out fishing. I had a canoe I'd made. The long boat had been gone for a few years. Suddenly there was the most god-almighty roar and it sounded like the island was bustin' apart. I tried to get back to shore but it was like the ocean was suckin' me out. I could see my family down on the shore callin' to me, and then I couldn't see nothin' the sky went so dark. It cleared a little and then there was another bang and the sea just roared and I thought I was dead for sure, but I didn't mind about myself, I just wanted to get back to Lani and the little ones. Then a wave pitched my canoe up high and I could see down to the beach, about a half a mile away. A wall of lava was rollin' down the mountainside as fast as you can think, and as I was watching it came down and over my family and into the sea. It made the water boil, and it hissed and spit as it turned to rock in the ocean.

I let the water carry me where it would. I didn't care no more.

Chapter Four

I don't know how long I was in that canoe. The sea was wild, and I couldn't get back to shore, and anyway, the whole island was on fire and there wasn't nothing to go back to no more. I think it must have been three or four days. It rained and I drank the rain water. I was lying in the bottom of the canoe waitin' to die when I heard voices speakin' English.

"It's an islander, look at those tattoos."

"That's no islander, he's got fair hair. It's a lost sailor. Ahoy, shipmate, are you alive or dead?"

"I might as well be dead," I said, sitting up, "but I'm alive."

I was taken on by an English ship on its way to the prison colonies of Australia. I had drifted west and they'd gone further east than they wanted to, or they'd a never found me. It felt strange to be with men again. The English were kind enough to me, which is more than they were to the poor prisoners they were taking to Australia. Some of them were there because they'd stolen a loaf of bread, and some were young enough to be called children.

The English are a stiff kind of people, but the prisoners were a lot of 'em Irish. They'd get to come up out of that stinkin' hold sometimes and we'd talk. Some of the hard cases used to ask me how far it was to those islands, and I think one or two had a mind to try to take the ship, but it warn't no use. There was a troop of marines on board, and they were a hard lot too. I didn't like to think what the prisoners would get once they got to Australia.

I didn't have no reason to live anymore, but since I was still alive after all I'd been through, I figured there must be some reason. When I got to Australia I sent a letter to Mary-Jane's sisters telling them all what I'd been through, and how I was trying to get back as soon as I could to see them and Ruthie. My little Ruthie would be ten years old, nearly. She didn't even know she'd had a brother and a sister, but they was dead now.

I couldn't get a ship to America right away, so I thought I'd look around Australia while I was there. I got work for a few days whenever I needed money. There didn't seem to be no shortage of jobs for a man to do, even with all them prisoners there.

We'd landed in Sydney, and that's where I stayed most of the time. There was all kinds of people there, prisoners and free, but the prisoners was most of 'em crazy to get back to England. Some of 'em though, who'd been there awhile and got their free papers, liked it, and stayed. The country was like no place I'd ever seen, and full of the most peculiar and strange animals. I never seen none like them anywhere else. Kangaroos, with their babies in pockets at the front, and things with ducks' feet and fur, and all kinds of strange things.

Well, it was a pretty country, one of the prettiest I'd ever seen. There was some mountains called the Blue Mountains that I took a look at. You couldn't get through, no how, but the road came up to a place where you could see. I went out there with a horse I hired. We passed road gangs, some of 'em in chains, and they was a pitiful sight. When I got up to the end of where the road goes, I tied up the horse and went wandering on a ways. I come out to an edge where you could look down. All there was for miles and miles was eucalyptus trees, so close together you couldn't see no ground anywhere. And there was a haze over it all on account of the oil them trees make seepin' up into the air. And birds! I never seen so many nor so many kinds, not even in the Sandwiches. Well I was standin' there just lookin' when I heard someone come runnin' up behind me. I turned quick and this wild lookin' feller comes barrelin' up.

"Don't say you've seen me!" he says and goes crashin' down through the trees. After a spell, I hear more runnin' and shoutin' and sure 'nough here come the soldiers runnin' down with their guns pointing.

"Have you seen a man come through here?" One says, sharp and suspicious.

"No, I ain't," I says, and right away he looks at me funny.

"Where you from?" he says.

"Well, Missouri, but I been a powerful lot a places in between."

"He's the American who washed up in Sydney, sir. Been living on the islands for ten years," someone says to him.

The first man looked a little less ready for a fight then, and says, "Well, watch out for anyone you see. There's a bushranger loose out here. Killed a constable up in Paramatta."

"I'll keep my eyes open sir," I says, nice as pie.

They all went back up the road way and I moseyd along toward the cliff edge. "They're gone," I said to the air.

After a minute or two the feller comes out. He'd been clinging to the brush under the cliff edge.

"Thank you sir," he said, not soundin' much like a murdering bushranger to me, but more like a well brought up gentleman. "I thought they had me then. If they catch me it's Van Dieman's land. Or the noose."

I heard about Van Dieman's land, so I knew why he was fearful. On the whole I think I'd a preferred the noose. "What they after you for? Escaped?" I asked, not lettin' on that I heard about him bein' a murderer.

"Yes, I escaped," he says, "but I killed one of them doing it. I was working in Paramatta as a clerk to the prison governor up there. I would have been given my papers within a year. One day I was walking through the settlement and I saw a constable flogging a young woman. She'd fallen down into the roadway and the monster was still beating her. Blood was running down her face and arms. I've seen horrors in this country, but that was my limit. I tried to make him stop and he pushed me away. Then I picked up a brick and stove his head in. I've been on the run ever since."

"You did right," I said.

We was both quiet for a minute. "What did you get sent out here for in the first place?" I asked him.

"Forgery," he says. "I was working in London. I was a lawyer. An old friend came and asked me to help him do something I knew was wrong. I let myself be persuaded and did it, and here I am." He laughed kind of bitter.

"What you going to do now?" I asked him.
"Stowaway on a ship if I can, get out of here and start again."
"Go back to England?"
"No, somewhere else. I'd be found if I went back to London."
"California?"
"I was thinking about that. Or Mexico."
"There's a ship in next month bound for California. I'm going to try to get on as a sailor. It's an American ship I hear, and wouldn't no one bother about you if you could get on board."

So we worked it out. I went back up there a few days later with some provisions for him. John Western his name was. Then again a week after. By that time the ship was in port. I got signed up as a sailor. The day before we were leaving, John Western snuck down to Sydney in the clothes of a free farm laborer. He wore a hat pulled down over his face and no one noticed him. He holed up that night in a stable and come four we got down near the harborside. There was a guard down by the ship. They was always watching for stowaways. I went out and got talking to him and give him a drink of some rum I'd got special. There wasn't much in the way or spirits in the colony, so he was grateful, I can tell you. Pretty soon I was pretendin' to be roarin' drunk, and he was the real thing. Then he passed out and I left the bottle there with him. It might be some comfort when he woke up, cause I knew he'd be in some trouble. John got up on the deck and then down into the hold where he hid himself. One of the mates was in on it and he gave us the wink. Truth was, lots of convicts got out that way, cause no man could bear to see the way they were treated down there. It wasn't human. It almost seemed too easy him gettin' away, but we did it. Come noontime we was watching Australia disappear behind us and a fair wind blowing for Polynesia. A day or two later John came out from hiding and just came to be one of the crew. I felt real good about it. Runaway niggers and runaway convicts. I was making a career out of law-breakin'.

Well, that trip back, it was fine. We stopped at Tahiti and then in the Sandwiches. John Western had to hide both times and not come out of the hold on account of the British always looking for runaways, so he missed those islands, but by and by we got to California. It was the year 1860, and I was thirty-one years old.

San Francisco had changed in the years I'd been away. It was a proper town now, no mud streets but pavements. And where the bars and whorehouses had been now there was grand buildings and fine-dressed people on the streets. I said goodbye to John and he said he reckoned he'd find something to do in Frisco, and I reckon he probably did. As for me, I went lookin' for the first overland to get me back to Arkansas.

Travelin' was easier. There was trains where there hadn't been none before, and almost ever' bit of country I went through was filled to burstin' with settlers. It made me feel kind of sad to think of all that empty land not being empty no more - kind of like seein' an animal in a cage. But people got to live somewhere I guess.

Well before I knew it I was back in St. Jo, and soon I was gettin' off the riverboat in St. Petersburg. Things had changed there too. Most all the old folks was dead and lots of the young ones had moved away west. Sid Sawyer was still there, but Susie Harper, who he'd married had got carried off by typhoid fever two years before. Sid had four little Sawyers he was a-bringin' up on his own, and I did feel sorry for him.

No one knew anything about Tom. He'd got back to Frisco and then come back home, but that was near eight years before. He'd hung around awhile and then gone off east, no one knew where. Aunt Polly had died the first year we'd gone west, so only Sid was left since Mary had married that northern school teacher who come through town. She was in New York somewheres. Sid knew where. I figured maybe Tom went there, but Sid said Mary'd've written if that was so, and I figured he was right.

I didn't stay around too long. I went to see my old nigger Jim, who was a free man now. He'd bought his wife and children and they was all free, and they'd stayed right there in St. Petersburg, not knowin' anywhere else much to go to. I told him all about the island I was stuck on all those years and he was mighty impressed. When I told him about Lani and the children, tears fell out of his eyes. He was the most soft-hearted nigger I ever knew, and the best.

After a few days I caught the riverboat and headed down to Arkansas. It felt mighty strange to be on that big river again after all that time. I knew every twist and turn, but some places had changed on the banks: towns where there hadn't been nothing; bigger towns where little ones had been before. And the people on the boat was different too. Time was, you'd catch a boat down south and ever' one you'd meet would be a farmer going to see his cousin, or a gambler goin' down to 'Orleans, or slaver. Now there was a lot more people looked like they was doing business. Talking close together in the saloon, or lookin' at maps on tables in the dining room. Somethin' was up, sure, but I didn't know what.

I finally got down there back to the old farm. I left the riverboat and walked the last mile or two down to the farm. There it was, lookin' pretty as a picture. The trees was all full of fruit, and the fields looked like they was ready to be harvested. There was a few nice lookin' cows munchin' in the paddock. Why it looked like paradise after what I'd seen and been through, and I just sat down and had a good cry before I could get the nerve to go up to the house and see ever' one. I was sittin' there on a log, kind of hidden, when I heard some footsteps. I looked around and there was a child lookin' at me from behind a bush. She was the prettiest child I'd ever seen, blue eyes, red cheeks, dark brown hair. I kind of figured who she was, but I didn't want to get my hopes up just yet.

"You sick mister?" she asked in that sweet little voice, "or hurt? I'll get my Ma and Pa if you want."

"Who's your Ma?" I asked, wipin' my eyes and trying to smile.

"Over yonder she is," she said, pointin', and I saw Susan there in the vegetable patch with another couple of little ones tumblin' around her feet.

"No, I'll come meet her myself," I said, "if you'll come with me." So I got up and we walked down the hill and over the paddock and on the way she just prattled on tellin' me ever' thing I wanted to know."

"I call her my Ma, but she's my aunt really. My real Ma died when I was born and my Pa was so broken hearted he run off to Californy and we thought he'd died, but Ma got a letter about a month ago from Australia that had gone to England afore it got here, sayin' he was there and that he was comin' back and wanted to see us all. He'd been lost on a desert island like Robinson Crusoe for all these years, and now he's comin' back!"

"Will you be glad to see him?"

"You bet, but I hope he don't want me to go off with him to no island, cause I like it fine here." She sounded a little worried when she said that.

"I don't think he would ever do no such thing, seeing how happy you are here," I said.

"No, I guess not."

About that time we'd come in view of the house and Susan looked up from her vegetables. She put her hand up to shade her eyes, and then she looked real careful, and then she started runnin'.

"It's Huck!" she yelled. "It's Huck, he's back!" And from all over the farm people come runnin'. The little girl she looked up at me.

"You my real father, then?"

"I am. Are you sorry?"

"No, I'm not!" she said and threw her little arms round my neck. I'd lost my little ones out there on that island, but this was almost like findin' them again.

Well, those was happy days. It was like being the prodigal son and raised from the dead all at the same time. I settled in back there and I was happy, and ever' one was happy to have me back. I got to workin' on the farm like old times and pretty soon I nearly forgot I'd been kidnapped and gone to sea, and shipwrecked, and seen a volcano blow up and island and take my wife and children away with it. It all seemed like someone else's life now that I was back home. But it was too good to last. I should a known it. Most things are.

It was 1860, and things was brewin'. We'd heard about the trouble in South Carolina, but no one expected the Carolinians to fire on Fort Sumter. We was southerners, sure, but we was Americans too. Lots of people didn't feel like I did, but lots of folks hadn't been around like I had, neither. And I never did have much truck with slavin' no how. Me and Mary-Jane hadn't had but one slave on the place, and he was treated real good. Susan and Bob had a couple, but they was real nice to them too. I knew there were places where that wasn't the way it was, though, and I secretly agreed with the abolitionists, havin' had a hand in that kind of thing myself when I was a boy. But I didn't tell no one how I felt.

So when war was declared and Bob and Joanna's husband run to join up, I kind of held back. Ever' one thought it was cause I was worn out from my adventuring, and I let 'em think that. I didn't want no part of killin'. I never did see no use in killin' people you don't know cause some general says you got to. It don't make no sense. And when the other men was gone, there was so much work to do on the farm. Those women couldn't a done it themselves, even with the niggers. So I just set still and waited. Like I said, I didn't much care what people thought 'bout me. I knew I was a man, even if I didn't go shootin' a lot of other men to prove it to myself. I'd seen a fair bit, and I think I knew the North would win. They had factories and big cities and ships and thousands of people. And what did we have? Pride, farms, and slaves. It wasn't no contest.

Joanna's husband he died at the second Bull Run battle, and Bob, he went at Fredericksburg. It was a bad, sad, terrible time. The south was losin' and I knew it was a goin' to lose, but after my two brothers-in-law died, I went and joined up. I can't rightly say why I did it. I'd left the farm in as good shape as I could. I knew those two niggers we had wouldn't run off like some had done. I said goodbye to Susan and Joanna and their children, then I went to find my little Ruthie.

She'd got to be a big girl since I got back, and she did favor her mother. I tell you, it just 'bout broke my heart saying goodbye to her, but I promised I'd be back, and I kept my word.

When I joined up things was for a change lookin' pretty good for the south. We was surgin' northwards and it looked like we might take Washington. People thought we might win, but I just thought, what do we do then? The country's too big for the south to run it. Truth was, nobody much thought about what would happen if we did win. Wars is like that. We just kept winnin' battle after battle. Leastaways that's what people were sayin'. I still didn't think we could win, but I just kept my mouth shut. First fight I was in wasn't much more than a skirmish, but it opened my eyes, I can tell you. We'd been marchin' for days and hardly sleepin' and hardly eatin'. Then we just stopped still for three days. We got so we wanted to march again just to have somethin' to do. Then we heard we was goin' to engage the enemy in the mornin'. I never seen no such chaos. Troops moved in about daybreak, the Yanks appeared over the top of a hill. At some signal ever' body starts shootin' and people start fallin' dead and wounded all around me. Now it's a fact that if you have to fight with someone, the only way to do it is up close so you know who you're hurtin'. If wars was fought with fists there'd be a lot less of 'em. If you can stand on a ridge a hundred feet away and pull a trigger and knock down and kill a man you don't know, and don't know his name, nor if he's got a wife or children, why you're less than an animal. You're like a rock fallin' off a cliff, or a bolt of lightning. War takes the human away from us. I know that's true. It happened to me too and I ain't proud it did.

But you get wrapped up in it, and me, I was shootin' at men I didn't know too, and killin' em. Seemed just about as soon as it got started that one was over. We'd lost about twenty-five and the Yanks about the same. We picked up our wounded and we went back to camp. I think the generals must a thought we was playing some big game. A few days later we marched on.

We had a few skirmishes on the way and then we crossed the border into Pennsylvania. It was summer and it was hot. By the time we got there we was wore out. We'd got to a place called Gettysburg.

You probably heard or read about that battle, but I can tell you, it wasn't like no battle. It was like the end of the world. Someone must have had some plan or other, but to me it just seemed like all hell broke loose and kept on goin'. I remember marchin' up and runnin' back, and shootin' till you couldn't see through the smoke. And horses rearing up through the smoke and dust like angels of destruction. And men fallin' down with their heads blown off. And bein' hungry and thirsty and hurt all at once. A Yank run at me with his bayonet, and him no more'n a boy, and I shot him dead, him who was some mother's pride and joy. It didn't make no sense.

We was with general Pickett's boys, and after the first day, things looked good. There was a quiet spell that evening and I left camp and wandered away. There was rubbish and blown up trees ever' where, and I could see where a little farm had been, but it was all blown to pieces. Down near what must a been the barn, I see a light flare and go out. Someone lightin' a pipe I figured. I had my pipe with me and I went down there. It was further than it looked and I was outside the lines, but I didn't know it till it was too late.

Even though there'd been fightin' all day, it was quiet out there. You could see how it had been a mighty pretty place before all this devilment had happened. I knew I shouldn't go no further, but I thought I might just have a smoke. I set down and lit my pipe. Then a bullet whizzed by my ear. I threw myself flat and said, "I'm a southerner, don't shoot."

"All the more reason," someone said.

I knew I was in for it then. I'd gone too far from the lines and got up to where the Yanks must a had their pickets. A minute passed, then the voice said,

"Where you from?"
"Arkansas."
"You don't sound like no Arkansas man."
"I come from Missouri, but I live in Arkansas. What's it to you, Yank?"

The voice went quiet. Why some Yank wanted to know where I was from was a mystery to me, but there was somethin' strange about that voice.

"Where in Missouri?"
"St. Petersburg."
"What's your name?"
"Finn."

I heard that man choke then sort of whistle, and I figured he was gettin' ready to blow my head off, but he says, almost in a whisper, "That you Huck? Glory be to God, I thought you was dead for sure!"

It was Tom Sawyer, and a stranger meetin' was never had, than the two of us, between the lines at the battle of Gettysburg. We didn't have much time, but I told him as quick as I could what had happened to me, and he told me his story.

After we'd split up in Hawaii, Tom he got a ship going back to California. She hit some rough weather and they was nearly lost, but finally they dragged back into Frisco. The first thing Tom did was to go find the Duke. I ain't sure what he thought he was goin' to do, but he was goin' to find him anyways. But when he got there, he was too late. That syndicate that had bought the Duke's salted mine had found him, and when Tom walked through the barroom door he sees a man raisin' a chairleg to hit someone layin' on the floor. I'm sure the Duke done some bad things, but don't no one deserve to die like that.

Then Tom got back to Missouri. He had some rough times gettin' there, but finally he made it back. But somehow once he was there it didn't seem so grand to be home. He'd gone away to see the world and less than two years later he was back where he started from. So he headed north. His sister had married a northerner, and he stayed with her a spell, then he headed off. Tom had gone to West Point for a couple of years when Judge Thatcher sent him, and he still knew some of the fellers, so he found a few of them. Some of 'em was soldiers, but one had left like Tom and was livin' in New York City. Tom bunked in with him and started lookin' for somethin' to do. He got into banking and then got into somethin' else. Nothin' much seemed to suit him though, so when the war broke out, he joined up in the army. They made him an officer right away on account of him bein' at West Point, even if it was only two years.

"But Tom," I said, "you're fightin' for the Yanks."
"The Yanks aren't any different than us, Huck, so what does it matter who you fight for? I'm fightin' for myself."

Well, I'd always listened to Tom Sawyer, but now I thought he was wrong, dead wrong. It was bad enough fightin' if you were fightin' for your own, but to fight for nothin', just to fight, wasn't right. And I told Tom so. He just sort of laughed.

"Someone's going to get something out of this war, Huck, and I aim to be one of them. I'm a captain already, and I aim to be a general before this show's through. I'm a general's aide and I'm mighty high in his estimation."

I looked at him there in the night and it was like seeing a ghost. He was a grown man with a moustache and a coat with gold braid on it, but a dead boy's eyes looked out of that face. Tom Sawyer was dead, and this man who wanted to get somethin' for himself out of people dying had replaced him. I turned to go.

"Wait Huck," he said.

"I got to get back," I said. But then Tom he kind of smiled and raised his gun toward me.

"No you don't, Huck." Then he sung out, "Pickets! Prisoner!" and two Yanks come runnin' up.

"Take this prisoner to the rear of the lines."

"Tom!" I almost screamed.

Tom turned away. "You'll live, Huck." He motioned towards the southern lines. "They aren't goin' to."

I was taken back of the lines where a lot of other miserable southern prisoners were. Then in the middle of the night someone comes along and shouts "Finn!" and I stand up.

"Come along with me."
"Where'm I goin'?"
"I don't know. General's orders."
They took me out of there and pretty soon I found myself somewhere a ways away from the battle lines. Someone comes out from between the trees pullin' a horse by the reins and hands it to me. He gives me a note and walks away. I opened it and all it said was, "Ride as far away as you can, as fast as you can. Tom."

I was way behind the Union lines and miles from my own. There wasn't no way I'd get back before daybreak, so I figured I'd better get away from there. I didn't want to get shot as no deserter, but I didn't want to get shot no how, so I headed west.

Well, I was a deserter now, and I would a been shot if they'd found me. Tom, he'd put some civilian clothes in the saddle bags, and fifty dollars in gold. I rode west. Soon as I was away from the battle, I was surprised how peaceful it was. Some little places I went through, folks didn't seem to know there was men killin' and dyin' not twenty miles away from them.

I knew I couldn't go home right away, but I sure didn't want the folks there to think I was killed. I figured they'd thought I was dead once though, and maybe they'd have to again. I heard the news in the town I passed through, that Gettysburg was over and that the South had lost. Lee lost more'n a third of his army, so I reckoned maybe Tom had saved my life. I thought about what I'd better do, and I figured maybe I'd make my way over to Ohio and then find my way back home. But I didn't have no real plan, not at all. I rode west for a couple of weeks, then I turned my horse's head south. I met some pretty rum customers along the way, I can tell you. War is like a river that washes all kinds of flotsam and jetsam into places where it ought to never be. But mainly the places I went through didn't have no soldiers in them, and pretty soon I was through Ohio and on to Indiana. Then Illinois, and finally I crossed the border back into Missouri. I had to be careful once I made it to Missouri because I was back in the south then, and I could get shot for desertion. When I got to St. Louis, there wasn't much traffic on the river, on account of the war, but I sold the horse and found me a boat would take me as far as Cairo. At Cairo I got another, and pretty soon I was rollin' down towards Arkansas. I watched St. Petersburg go by, but I didn't get off the boat. There wasn't nothin' there for me no more.

When I got back to our farm, they near jumped out of their skins. I walked into the kitchen one evenin' at suppertime, and you'd a thought I was a ghost. When they didn't hear from me, they thought I was killed at Gettysburg, and not found. I told them I'd found Tom Sawyer in the battle, and that he was fightin' for the Yanks.

I lay pretty low the next few months. The war was goin' from bad to worse, and lots of men was goin' home, but there was still trouble if you were caught. I got back to runnin' the farm, and one day we heard it was all over. The men came stragglin' back one or two at a time. Many a one came to our door and asked for a drink of water or a meal. The South was on its knees, completely crushed, and all for what? The niggers was freed, but half of 'em was starvin' and had no place to go. We were just about alright, but times was hard. Besides me and Ruthie, there was Susan and her three little ones, and Joanna and her boy. The two niggers had gone.

Taxes was high and got higher. Ever' thing got more expensive, but we were lucky. It had always been a small farm, so we could run it ourselves. And by and by Joanna got married again to a one legged man who'd been at Chancellorsville. By 1869 we was back on our feet, and I'd been back near as long as I'd been away. Then my little Ruthie got hitched with a boy from town. She was nineteen by then and just as pretty as her mother had been. I was real proud of her. After she got married she moved to town so I didn't see her as much, and I figured maybe it was time for me to move along too.

The farm was doin' just fine. I knew ever' one could get along without me. Thing was, Ruthie had her own life, and Susan and her children had theirs, and Joanna, she had hers. I wanted to be around while Ruthie was growin' up, but now she was grown. I was forty years old, and I felt an itch to move again. And truth to tell, since I'd lost Mary-Jane, I never did feel properly settled nowhere. So in 1870, I packed my bag, I give my new grandson a kiss, I waved goodbye to them all, I caught the riverboat up to St. Louis, and I headed out west.

Chapter Five

Funny thing about the West, it's almost like you think about it more than you live in it. For the last couple of years before I left the farm, I'd been thinkin' about headin' west, and then when I was doin' it, it almost seemed like the thinkin' about it had been more real than the actual doin'.

There was still quite a lot of Indian trouble in those days, and I reckoned I'd avoid it, but one way and another I found myself headin' for the Dakotas. There was rumor of gold in the Black Hills, but wasn't no gold rush yet - that came later. I stayed on the river as long as I could, then I took to horse. There's some powerful pretty country up there, and some strange places too. The first time I went, it was late spring. The snow was just about gone, but it was still pretty cold. There's a place up there the Indians just call "bad lands" and nothin' lives there except coyotes and rabbits, I reckon. I passed through that way. I never seen anything like it. All tumbledown rock and nothin' alive at all, like God just said, "I <u>don't like</u> this place," and just blasted it. After the bad land, the Black Hills was a sight to see. The Indians call them black, but really they're just the darkest green you ever saw.

I knew there was Indian trouble around the Black Hills, but I wasn't lookin' for none. I expect it was foolishness, but it ended up, well, you'll see how it ended up in the end. Anyway, I was passin' through that country. I thought I'd get up towards the Canada line where there was rumor of gold. I kept away from where I thought the Indians were, but they found me. One day I was riding along between a couple of hills when I notice something up on a ridge. Then I notice somethin' on the other side, and while I'm looking, up comes hoofbeats from behind. I was surrounded in a minute by some of the meanest lookin' Indians I'd ever seen. They just rode along with me and by and by we come to their village. I figured I was a goner, and I just hoped they wasn't goin' to put themselves to too much trouble killin' me. There was a chief sittin' down lookin and a whole crowd all around shoutin' and hissin'. I was standin' there wonderin' what was goin' to happen next, and not much wantin' to think about it when one of the braves that captured me come up and grabbed the collar of my shirt and ripped it down.

Well you never heard quiet take over from sound quite so quick. That brave he gasped, then he rips the back of my shirt too and I'm standing there bare from the waist up. He kind of steps back away and drops his arms. Maybe you remember how I said that Lani had tattooed me. My family at home, they'd got used to it, but whenever strangers came I always put on a shirt and buttoned it up, cause folks tended to be shocked. Well, these Indians was pretty near amazement. Lani had spent considerable time on those tattoos, and it's fair to say that hardly an inch of my chest or back that wasn't covered with some outlandish symbol or picture. I didn't think much about it most of the time, but I could see I'd made quite an impression. I thought I'd better make the best of it, so I kind of turned and glared at the Indian who'd ripped my shirt, then I walked over, quite calm, to the chief and I sit down and pull my pipe out of my trouser pocket and light up. Well, you probably know, you share a pipe with an Indian and you ain't got to worry anymore. After than I was just kind of taken in. A few days later they packed up that camp and moved on, and I moved on with 'em. I didn't have no other plans. The Indians, they treated me with sort of awe at first, at least the grown ones, but the children they was just curious. I'd take off my shirt and let 'em have a look whenever they wanted. They called me The Painted Man, and I guess that's what I was. I noticed one time when I was washin' that brave who'd been the one ready to kill me, watchin'. I think he was waitin' to see if it washed off. He must of been real disappointed when it didn't.

There was some trouble in those days, with miners comin' in to Indian lands up there in the Dakotas, but not like it got later. The tribe traveled north a ways, after buffalo, and I reckon we went over the Canadian border a few times back and forth.

Those plains up there are something. I've stood on a hilltop at sunset and looked out over somethin' that looked like the ocean, if the ocean was grass, all wavin' in the wind, goin' on forever. Like I said when I was a sailor, it makes you feel like you know what people mean when they talk about God when you see land like that. And nothin' had lived there except Indians and buffalo for thousands of years. And they got along fine. The Indians never killed no more buffalo than they needed. One of the things they hated most about the white man was his wasting ways. White men come in and kill more buffalo than they can eat. The Indians may be savage, but they just didn't understand that.

That young brave that wanted to kill me at first, by the end we got to be friends. Story was round the camp that his mother had seen a horse go plumb loco just after he was born. That's how he got his name. I rode out with him and some others a few times huntin'. I'd got used to usin' a bow when I was on my island, and when the Indians saw how I could shoot with it - I used to shoot fish sometimes, stead of usin' a hook or spear - they got real respectful. I hadn't had much cause to use a bow since I'd been back, so I was a little rusty at first, but it come back pretty quick.

I stayed with those Indians all through the spring and summer was long gone before I left them. The first snow flakes were beginnin' to fall when I saddled up. That brave, Crazy Horse he was called, he rode with me a week till we got near the settlements, then we smoked a pipe together and said goodbye. I watched him ride off and I felt like I was watchin' the dead pass away, cause even then it as clear to anyone that there was no way the Indians were goin' to last in a white man's world.

Winter was comin' on hard, and I reckoned I'd head south. It gets a mite chilly up in the Dakotas country once the leaves have fallen. I headed back the way I'd come and in a week I was headin' back through the Black Hills. I got down into Nebraska in another couple of weeks.

That country was fillin' up faster than you could think. Even with winter comin' on there was still wagons loadin' up and settin' off for further west, and plenty that was stayin' right there. It made me shiver to think of them poor folks livin' through the winter in those sod houses that was the best they had if they had anything. The fellers had a kind of hard look about them, but the women, they just looked defeated. I'd see 'em, standin' in their doorways, if you could call 'em doorways, lookin' out over that big, wide empty prairie they'd decided to call home. They must a wondered what they were doin' there, miles from anyone and anywhere, and the Indians still pretty lively too.

I got down into Kansas, and I thought I'd head down and have a look at Texas, but I got caught up in some trouble. This is what happened. I rode into a little Kansas town one afternoon. I went and found the telegraph office to send a telegram to Ruthie that I was alright and doin' fine. After that I went to find somethin' to eat and a place to clean up and stay the night. I'd been on the road a fair few days and I was fairly worse for wear. I was just sat down in the barbershop with the soap all over my face when it sounded like a herd of wild horses was comin' down main street. The barber turns and looks out the window and says, "Oh my God, it's the James gang!"

I'd heard of the James gang. No one who lived in Kansas or Arkansas or Oklahoma or Missouri could feel safe of them. But they weren't likely to bother farmin' folks like we were in Arkansas. It was towns with banks, and telegraph offices, and railroads they went for. And now they was here. They came roarin' down the main street, five of 'em on five of the finest horses I ever seen. The little one, he was Jesse. Those horses wheeled around and then four of 'em jumped off and left the fifth man with the horses. They headed straight to the bank across from the barber shop. I heard a couple of shots, then they come out, walkin' not runnin'. They was in no hurry and looked like they weren't too worried 'bout anything. Jesse, he stopped and looked over at the barbershop. He kind of rubbed his cheek and then he came on in. I saw one of the others sayin' somethin' to him, but he just laughed. Three of 'em stayed outside, but Jesse and another man came right in. There was only one chair in there, so when Jesse said he wanted a shave, I got right up. I started to leave, but Jesse says, "This won't take long. You just wait." And then he sits down comfortable and tells the barber to start shavin' him.

That barber was shakin' so hard I don't know how he did it without drawin' blood, but he managed. Then Jesse said he'd like his hair cut too. I was just standin' there watchin'. He looks at me after a minute and says, "What you lookin' at friend?" Well, I just said what I was thinkin', not havin' no cause to do otherwise, and said, "You're a Missouri man, ain't you?"

"I am," he says, "what's it to you?"

"I am too," I said. I knew Jesse'd been in the war, so I asked him which regiment he was in and we got to talkin'. It was a friendly sort of conversation to be havin' with a famous outlaw. Pretty soon his hair was cut and one of the fellers outside yells somethin'. Jesse slammed down a twenty dollar gold piece and jumped for the door. Within a minute they couldn't be seen for dust, and not a minute later the marshall and his men come ridin' in. Well, after the coolness of those outlaws, the marshall and his men looked like schoolboys. They went ridin' off after them, but after a couple of hours they come back.

That night I was standin' in the saloon havin' a drink when one of the marshall's men comes up to me. "I hear you were pretty friendly with James when he was here."

"Oh, I was just talkin'," I said.

"You sent a telegram 'bout an hour 'fore they got here, didn't you?"

"I thought telegrams was private," I says.

He kind of laughs, "Touchy, ain't you? Who was it to?"

"My daughter," I said.

Then he really laughs. "Your daughter! Then how come the James boys knew that the marshall was out of this town huntin' the Brown gang today, when everybody knew there was railroad money in the bank for the payrolls?"

"You tell me," I said, and I downed my whiskey and went out.

He calls after me, "You'd better watch out who you talk to and who gets your telegrams, mister."

I thought nothin' more of it and went back to the hotel and went to bed, but 'bout the middle of the night there was a hammerin' at the door like a fire or something. I got up and opened it and there was a crowd includin' the marshall and the man from the bar. I didn't have no shirt on and I forgot about my tattoos, so when they seen me they all kind of gasped.

"Lord almighty, what is he?"
"Some kind of heathen savage. I hear he lived with the Hunkapapas up north."
"These ain't Indian," I said, "I got 'em in the south seas. I used to be a sailor."
That seemed to quieten 'em down, but then the marshall he says, "Put your clothes on and lead us to your friends."

"I ain't got no friends in Kansas," I said. All my kin are in Arkansas and Missouri.

"You know what I mean. You lead us to the James boys or you'll find that pretty hide of yours hangin' from the end of a rope."

Well, there ain't no point to argue with people in that state. They were a mob, and a mob don't have no brain, just fists, so I put my clothes on and come quiet. We saddled up and set out. It was just past midnight and there was a nice moon out to ride by. We just mosey'd along for awhile, then the marshall says, "Which way we go?"

"You tell me," I says, "I don't know."
"Don't you give me none of that. Are they over towards the south ridge in those caves above the river?"

"I guess so," I said.

We rode on a ways and someone says, "I see a fire!"

We went ridin' up like hell for leather and found the fire, and some poor travelin' folk. I reckon they was headed out west and thought it was Indians after them. There was a man and his wife and a couple of little boys. The man was standin' there with a rifle and the little boys had grabbed a shovel and a hoe from the wagon. They'd been asleep and the woman was in the wagon cryin'. The marshall he muttered somethin' and we moved off. We rode another couple hours and then someone else says, "Smoke up in the trees."

We went in real slow then. When we was near the marshall says to me, "You go in, real friendly now, and see your chums."

I didn't like the sound of an ambush like that at all. And like as not I'd get killed in the crossfire, so when I get down off my horse, I just snag him with my boot. He whinnied and I seen a movement up ahead and I knew it would be alright. I went walkin' in and sure 'nough it was the James boys, but they knew what was up, and I tried to signal with my eyes what was goin' on. Jesse he read me and he shouts, "Who in tarnation are you! Get out a here unless you want a belly full of lead!"

'Bout that time the rest of the gang had worked their way around our boys, and pretty soon the shootin' begun. I dropped down to the ground and in a minute it was all over. Six men dead includin' the marshall, and the James boys didn't have a mark on nary a one of 'em. Well I felt pretty sick. All them men that had been live were lyin' there in their own blood. I'd seen worse, in the war, but it don't make no difference.

Frank he asked what I was doin' with that gang, and I explained how they'd mistook me for one of them. "Well, you better come along with us now," Jesse said, "cause your life ain't worth nothin' in Kansas."

I didn't want to be no outlaw, even though I'd had a tolerable history of bein' outside the law, what with runaway niggers and escaped convicts and desertin' from the army. I said no one in that town even knew my name, and no one had seen me much except that gang that was now all dead, so I'd get on my way. It wasn't far to Colorado, so I figured I'd head out that way. I was runnin' low on money and there was a silver strike somewhere I heard. Jesse he just sort of nodded. Then I went back and got my horse. The rest of 'em we just set loose. I reckoned they'd find their own way home. Trouble was, I'd left my money and the rest of my clothes back in the hotel, and I didn't want to go back to that town, no how. Jesse he must a known what I was thinkin', cause he says, "Wait a minute," and hands me up a little bag. I didn't look at it till later, but there was more'n three hundred dollars in gold there, cash money.

I left them outlaws and headed towards Colorado. It was gettin' cold, and the further I got up in those mountains, the colder it got. I was glad of Jesse's money, no matter how it was got. I got up to Leadville 'bout the end of November. I never seen such a rough town. There was miners and outlaws and railroad men and storekeepers all mixed up together. It was like California had been back in '50, but a mite rougher. There was a hangin' ever' day or two, and shootin's just about ever' night. I got fixed up with some fellers who had a claim and needed more men to work it. They had about twenty-five of us minin' and they paid good. It was two brothers, an older one and a young feller about nineteen. There was a syndicate trying to buy them out, but these boys wanted to hold on. It looked to me like a good claim, too, and they had got a tunnel sunk right down into it. One day I was down there workin' and I hear this knock-knock noise through the rock. I got back to the main shaft and found one of the other miners and he come too. We both listened and heard it, sure as anything, like someone was just there on the other side of the rock wall.

"I bet it's that syndicate," the other miner said, "trying to break through and then claim this tunnel's theirs."

I knowed he was right, so we both headed up and found the older brother who was really the boss. The young feller comes in while we were talkin' and hearin' it, he grabs a rifle and runs to the shaft. His brother tried to stop him, but he called the elevator operator to let him down before his brother could stop him. By the time we got down there it was all over. The syndicate's miners had broke through all right, and when they did they met a rifle in their faces. The younger brother told them to turn back or he'd shoot. They made like they were going to and then one of 'em turned back and shot him with a pistol before anyone knew what had happened. They high-tailed it back, but now the younger brother was dead. The older one sat there on the floor of that shaft cradling his younger brother and just weepin' like a woman.

After that happened I figured I'd had enough of Leadville. Trouble was the snow was pretty thick and gettin' out on the stage a mite risky. But I took it anyway. My horse had long died. The altitude gets 'em. That stage ride was somethin' I ain't likely to forget soon. The driver just drove like wildcats was after him, and more'n once we skidded near that edge and could you could see all the way to the bottom of Colorado from up there. We finally made it down though, and I headed for Denver.

Denver had got to be quite a city on the money comin' down from the mines, and the railroad was through. I used the rest of the pay I had left and caught the train out to California. I hadn't been in California since I'd got back from the islands, and it was hardly the same place at all anymore. Frisco was nothin' like the wild place it had been in '50, or even '60. There was mansions up and down the streets, and street cars and well dressed people ever' where. You couldn't hardly see the ocean anymore, less you went right down to the beach. I caught a ferry boat and went on up-country. There was people and buildin' goin' on that way too, and I reckoned there wasn't no place safe from progress.

I traveled around a bit too. It was pretty country round there. Up in the Napa valley, they'd put in a lot of vines in some places, and there was a winery up there all made of stone and run by some kind of French monks. So Europe was comin' over too. It was a pretty place, no denyin' but it seemed strange. I stayed up that way a few months, needin' work, and there bein' plenty of it about, and then I thought maybe I'd mosey down towards Texas, not havin' been there before. I wanted to see if there wasn't some place left that was still wild before it all got taken over by houses and farms and people. I headed back to Frisco, then went down the coast towards Los Angeles before I headed inland.

That coast road, it gets pretty wild in places. It was winter still, so there was plenty of water fallin' out of the sky and blowin' up from the sea, and by the time I made Los Angeles, I was one sick man. I found me a room in a little place run by a Mexican gal and her daughters. She had about six of 'em, and I couldn't tell one from the other. She was a widow, the Mexican lady, and her name was Juanita. Well, when I arrived I was coughin', and pretty soon I was ravin' and feverish. Juanita, she looked after me as though I was her own family, not just some vagabond who'd turned up at her front door. I was sick for near a month. If it hadn't of been for that Mexican gal, I'd a died, sure. After a month, I was sittin' outside in the sunshine one morning, fixing a toy what belonged to one of them daughters. I told Juanita that I was fixin' to get work soon as to pay her back for all she'd done for me. This day she come out and sit down beside me. We got to talkin' and she said why didn't I just stay around there with them and work for her. She needed a man to do things around the place, and there was a little bit of land at the back that needed some attention payin' to it. I didn't have no real plans, and still being weak, I said yes.

I stayed in a little room out at the back once I was completely better, and more or less became part of the family. That was a lively household, I can tell you, with Juanita and all them girls. I learned Spanish pretty quick too. I did all the heavy work around the place. There hadn't been a man around since Juanita's husband had run off and left her four years before - she called herself a widow, but no one knew if her husband was dead or not - and there was plenty to do. I thought he must have been one blamed fool, cause even with that

pack of children to run her down, and all the work of keepin'
boarders in the house, she was still a good lookin' woman.

After about six months, I was sittin' outside one evenin' smokin' my
pipe and lookin' at the stars. I could smell the sea air and the evening
was balmy. I thought I was in about as good a place as I was likely to
find, and I liked Juanita and the girls, I liked 'em just fine. So I said to
her, as I was a widower and she was a widow, would she like to get
hitched and just make it legal. She looked kind of sad and smiled. She
said she'd like to, but her and Fernando, they'd been married by a
priest and she'd have to know he was dead before she could take up
with anyone else. I couldn't argue with that, and a few weeks later
when I come home one day, I heard all kind of ruckus in the yard. I
went out, and there was Fernando, a good-lookin' feller, out in the
yard, with all the girls sittin' on him and talkin' to him and fussin'
over him. And there was Juanita standin' by the kitchen door with
those black eyes of hers just shinin'. So I packed my things and left.
Wasn't no reason to cause problems.

I'd been with them since early spring, and now it was gettin' on for
winter again. Not that winter in those parts is much to think about. It
hardly ever even gets cold enough to put a coat on. I was sorry to
leave that family, but I didn't mind gettin' out on the road again. I
wandered down as far as San Diego, then on up into Arizona. There
was still a lot of Indian trouble in those parts, and I was afraid of
runnin' into Apaches cause ever' one knew what they was like. I
didn't want to end up losin' my hair, so I figured I'd head back up
towards Denver and maybe try my hand at minin' again. On the way
up I run into a surveyor and his team who was settin' out to ride
down the Colorado through the big cañon, and I traveled with them
a ways. We passed through that country, and it was fine. I don't
hardly have words to describe how it was, but it was somethin'
thinkin' that river had carved through and made that cañon just like
a knife carvin' through butter. It makes you think. There ain't nothin'
stronger than nature, no matter what. I seen cannons and explosions,
and all manner of things man can make to make himself feel strong,

but there ain't nothin' stronger than that trickle of water that cuts through rocks and takes its time to do it.

I got up to Denver and I settled in there for the winter. I had written to Ruthie from ever' where I stopped, but since I'd left Los Angeles she hadn't had no place to write back to. So after a month in Denver I got a letter from her tellin' me that Susan, my wife's sister had died. I felt bad I hadn't known about that, and I made up my mind to go back and see them all. I'd been away a couple of years. So when spring come, I was ridin' that riverboat out of St. Louis, headin' back down to Arkansas. I'd stopped in St. Petersburg, but there weren't hardly any of the folks I'd known anymore. The war had changed all that. There were a lot of new folks and even northerners moved in too. No one had heard about Tom Sawyer, and I kept it quiet that he'd been fightin' for the north. Sid had heard rumor of it from Mary, but no one knew for certain. Sid thought maybe he'd gone to Europe, but no one knew for sure.

Well, I got back to Arkansas and saw ever' one at the farm, and my Ruthie and her family who lived in town. She had three little ones and that house was full of the most amazing caterwaulin' and goin' on that you'd be likely to hear. I stayed for awhile, then I went back out to the farm and moved back in.

It was good to be back, and there was plenty to do, so I stayed. I figured my adventurin' days was over. It was 1873, and I was near 43 years old.

Chapter Six

The next few years went by like the wind. I worked on the farm and watched the children grow up. Ruthie and her husband came back from town so we had the whole family there; them and me, Susan's children, and Joanna's family. There was two farmhouses there since me and Mary-Jane had built the second one when we was first married, so there was room for ever' one. Louisa and her family and Susan's children lived in the newer farmhouse and Ruthie's lived in the old one. I had built myself a little cabin away from the rest. I always did like a solitary life.

Things went along just fine for a couple of years, then we hit some bad luck. Louisa's eldest boy fell in the river and was drowned. Then they raised the taxes on the farm, which we owned, and we had to put it under mortgage. Things went from bad to worse and in 1875 the cotton crop failed. It looked like we might lose the farm. Those damn carpetbaggers had just about ruined the south after the war, but we had always managed, it bein' a family farm and not any hired labor. I didn't know what we would do, and then I heard about the gold strike up in Dakota. I knew a bit about minin' and it sounded like this was a good one. They said there was nuggets just layin' on the ground in the Black Hills. I'd been in the Black Hills too, and I reckoned maybe I could get in before the rest and make a strike. So that's what I did.

I took the river boat back up to St. Louis and headed to Deadwood. It was stage most of the way, and the Indians keepin' things mighty warm. You never seen such a wild place, and even Leadville looked like a Sunday school picnic next to it. It seemed like ever' last chance no-hoper in the whole country had ended up there lookin' for gold, so it wasn't no surprise when the second night I was there I walked into a saloon and who should I find but Tom Sawyer.

Tom, he'd been around, and I must say, he looked a little worse for wear. He always had liked a drink, and now he liked it a little more than it liked him. After the war, he'd gone back to New York, but couldn't settle to nothin' there. He thought he'd get somethin' out of that war, but he got nothin'. His general got shot and Tom was just one of a hundred captains lookin' for somethin' to do. Then like Sid thought, he went to Europe. He didn't go to London though, he went to some little place that was havin' a war and got in on the side that would pay him most. It was like Tom Sawyer still thought it was some kind of a game. He went from one country to another, and he'd just got back to America that month. He'd headed right out to the goldfields when he heard about the strike. I did thank him for savin' my hide at Gettysburg, even if the way he did it wasn't what I'd've done.

Funny thing was, there was still a glimmer of the old Tom under all that brass he put on. He was powerful glad to see me. There was no hidin' that. The thing was, Tom was a good boy, a real good boy, but he thought that life was just a game. Even with all the fightin' and killin' and dyin' he'd seen, it was still a game. I didn't understand how no one could go through things without them touchin' him somewheres. But Tom, he was like that. I don't like to think he meant no harm, it was just like some part of his heart wasn't there.

Well, we set up together and decided we'd go into the gold fields as a team. The soldiers had been tryin' to keep the prospectors out, but they was gettin' in now, and the Sioux was mighty stirred up. Tom didn't worry too much, but I knew the Sioux. I had lived with them a spell, and I knew when they meant business, they meant it. So we got together a set-up, and for a little while, it was like old times. Tom and me made a couple of strikes, and after a couple of months I'd made enough to pay the taxes back home and a little over. That was enough for me, so I cashed in and headed off, but Tom, he stayed.

I headed home and got the bailiffs off the farm. Just about then we got word of big trouble in the Indian territory. Seemed like the prospectors had really riled up the Indians, and they was on the warpath. There'd been some killin' and there was more to come. I was glad I wasn't there, but I was worried about Tom.

One afternoon I was out in the orchard prunin' one of the pear trees when up runs one of my grandsons, the younger one. He was holding a telegram and it looked like he'd run most of the way from town with it. It was so crumpled up I couldn't hardly read it, but I made it out. It was from Tom. It said: "Big strike our claim. Come immediately. Tom". Well, it was like the old Tom to let me know, and it made me glad that he hadn't just kept it to himself. I wondered about goin' for a day or two, but then somethin' happened that made up my mind.

I was up on the hill behind the farm seein' to some fencin' when I heard voices coming from down below by the roadway. It was McGowan, the carpetbaggin' Irishman who was tax-collector now. He was with some other feller. The other feller said,

"I thought we had them. No one could have come up with that money so fast."

Then McGowan spoke. "It's that god-damned Finn. He's half savage anyway. I don't know how he does it but he always scrapes through. we'll get it this time though."

"Prettiest farm I ever saw," the other man said.

"The taxes next spring will finish them. Even Finn won't be able to come up with the amount of money they'll have to pay."

They laughed and said somethin' else I didn't hear and then walked back down the hill to where they had a buggy waitin'. I knew I had to go back to Dakota.

Ruthie and the others, they weren't happy about me goin', but they knew I could look after myself, so a week later I was ridin' that riverboat again, headin' for the goldfields. Susan's boy Rab come along with me. I got back to Deadwood and found Tom. Our claim had struck big, and Tom was busy fightin' off all comers. We spent a couple of months diggin' her out, then we sold 'er to a syndicate. I sent Rab home with my share. I knew they'd be alright now, for at least a couple more years. And I'd heard rumors too, that those northerners who'd come down to bleed the south dry after the war wasn't goin' to be around a lot longer.

I don't know if I was fixin' to go back, or to go on. But Tom, he was restless and I figured I would stick with him awhile. About then, the cavalry come through Deadwood, and Tom ran into a feller he knew from the war. He was a captain and had been with Tom at Gettysburg. He took him off to meet the rest of the soldiers and when Tom come back he says, "I'm goin' to ride with them, Huck." And I knew that I'd be ridin' out alone, whichever way I went.

Tom, he went off with the cavalry, and I stayed around a while. I don't know if you've ever seen the Black Hills, but they are one of those places you can understand people dyin' for. The Sioux was all gone from them, mainly, out on the warpath, and the prospectors was diggin' and ruinin' everything, but there was still places you could go to see what it ought to be like. I packed up and thought I'd head home again, and I was passin' through on my way. The Indians say those hills are full of the spirits of their ancestors, and I can believe it. I climbed up a little ridge and come down through the trees into a clearing. But then I stopped dead. There was a Sioux there, and he wasn't no ghost. He was doin' somethin' and then he heard me. He turned and I thought I was gone. I didn't have no gun with me. He comes runnin' up to me with a knife out and then suddenly he stops. He looks at me for a minute or two, then he smiles. He signals for me to open my shirt, and when he sees them tattoos, he laughs. "Painted Man!" he says in English, and I knew I was alright. It was my friend from before, Crazy Horse.

I rode with Crazy Horse back to his people. They thought I was a prisoner at first, then Crazy Horse tells them who I was. I had to show my tattoos again. Seems I'd become somethin' of a legend among them and even the children knew about the Painted Man.

They were havin' bad times. The army had broken ever' treaty it made with them and they knew they was hunted. Yellow Hair was after them, and that was bad. I couldn't do nothin' to help, but after I see them all and hear how bad it was, I couldn't go back to the white men, not then.

We heard of battles and skirmishes to the south and east. We was up near Rosebud Creek then. Sitting Bull was with us, and it looked like big trouble comin'. It was strange bein' with the Sioux. Even though it was dangerous and I knew I might die with them, I felt peaceful, more peaceful than I'd been for a long time. I can't rightly explain why. There was just somethin' that felt like a circle bein' finished. They figured I was more Indian than white, 'specially on account of bein' painted up the way I was, and when I was dressed in Indian clothes, you couldn't tell much difference between us.

It's wide and lonesome up in that country, and full of spirits, the Indians say. I've stood on a hilltop at sunset and just felt it all wash right through me. It's like the land is alive, though most people don't think of it like that. The Indians do, and they understand it, and bein' with them, I got to understand it too. There's somethin' powerful about land that ain't been touched by people. Oh, the Indians lived on it, but they didn't really change it, or spoil it like white folks do. What I mean is, where there's country that ain't been changed, or lived in, it's like seeing what God made for the first time. I never rightly understood it till I was with the Sioux again.

While we were there the Indians did their sun dance. It was somethin' they don't do very much, and Sittin' Bull had a vision of the white men fallin' upside down into the Sioux camp. He'd cut himself to make that vision come, and he'd lost a lot of blood.

One day I was out huntin' and when we got back into camp, late, there was all kinds of ruckus goin' on. There'd been a battle while we were out. The braves I was with were mad they'd missed it, but I was happy I wasn't there. Some soldiers had come and there'd been a fight, mostly a stand-off, but bigger trouble was comin'. Sitting Bull was still too weak to fight, but Crazy Horse had been in the battle. We packed up then and headed for the Greasy Grass, that river the whites call the Bighorn.

I never seen so many Indians in one place as was there. They was comin' from ever' where, Sioux, Cheyenne, even Crow. When we finally got to the Greasy Grass river, there must have been eight or ten thousand there. A lot of 'em had come up from the agencies to fight for their land back. There was men, women and children there. I never seen such a crowd.

We was there a few days, and more and more Indians comin' in. Some of 'em looked at me strange and dangerous, so I took to walkin' around without my shirt on so they could see I was as heathen as they were. It was hot enough anyway. Then word came. there was cavalry approachin'.

I told Crazy Horse I couldn't kill no white men, no matter what I thought of 'em. So it was sure battle was goin' to start, I slipped away and got to where I could see what was happenin'. The first thing that happened was that a smaller force came at the camp from one side. There wasn't no braves there and they commenced to killin' women and children. White men or no, I couldn't stand that and I run out of where I was hid in time to shoot a couple of them bastards. Then the braves all come runnin' and I got clear. I knew there was plenty of Indians didn't know who I was, and could mistake me for one of the enemy, so I stayed clear when I could. Some of them soldiers got away, but the next thing, all the braves was runnin' the other way to a ridge. Yellow Hair had brought his troops over that way and the Indians was goin' to get them. From out of nowhere, Crazy Horse showed up. "Come with me, Painted Man," he said, "or you will die." I jumped up behind him on his horse and we rode down toward the battle. About a half a mile away he stopped and I got off. I was away from the village and the battle. "Stay here," he said. Crazy Horse was right. I would've got killed in the village by some Crow or Cheyenne. Only the Sioux knew I was their friend, and not even all of them.

I watched that battle from there, and it was a terrible sight to see. Those soldiers was completely outnumbered. Yellow Hair was a fool to have tried to fight them, but ever' one knew that George Custer was braver than smart. As I was watchin' the battle I saw someone break out of the cavalry lines. He was ridin' and lookin' around wild, tryin' to see which way to go. He wasn't in no cavalry uniform, and then I saw. Three Indians come up behind him and one on the side. He didn't stand no chance, but he would've died either way. The knocked him off his horse and one of 'em got out his scalping knife. I felt cold and sick and I put my head down and closed my eyes. Even from where I was I could see it was Tom Sawyer, and I never thought I'd see him die like that. That battle was over before it begun, and the squaws was out their cuttin' up the soldiers before they was even cold, and some of 'em not dead. I seen soldiers put their revolvers in their mouths and pull the trigger when they seen how it was goin' to end.

Crazy Horse he did come and find me after it was all over, but I didn't go back with him. I rode west. A couple of Sioux came with me a ways. When I was out of Indian country they went back, and I rode on. I didn't care if I was live or dead no more. I rode west.

Chapter Seven

It was 1876. America hadn't even been a country but a hundred years, and look at the mess we was in. Northerners and Southerners still hated each other. The Indians was on the warpath and on the way to bein' wiped out forever. Didn't seem right to me that all that hope and believin' should come to that. I guess I really never was much of a good American though. Why I'd helped a runaway slave when I wasn't much more'n a boy. And I'd lived with more'n one kind of savage, and didn't find no harm in 'em. So after I saw the battle at the Greasy Grass, I decided I probably wasn't even white no more, and I headed out.

I spent a long time out on those plains. It was hot that summer, and I didn't even need no blankets at night when I'd fall asleep. I run into a few Indians here and there, but most of 'em knew about the Painted Man, and if they didn't, sayin' a few words in Sioux usually convinced 'em I wasn't no enemy. The army was after the ones who'd killed Custer and the boys, and the Indians was heading north. I kept out of the way, mainly. I just wanted to be by myself for a spell.

Like I said before, there's something about those plains. It almost felt like being out on the ocean again. You can see pret' near forever up there, and you can <u>feel</u> forever. I don't know how else to say it. You ride along in the hot sun and pretty soon you ain't sure which is the sky and which is the ground, and then you realize that it don't make no difference and you're just in the middle of it, and whatever it is is like the whole world opening up and showin' itself to you, but no words can say what you've seen. I guess I'd lived with the Indians and Lani enough to know that the land keeps secrets that you can't ever know except you become part of it. I know it don't sound like it makes no sense at all, but if you ever been out there like that, you'll maybe know what I mean.

I fell in with some trappers headin' for Canada one evenin'. They weren't much bothered by the Indians and they was more'n half savage themselves. Wasn't either of 'em had seen a razor blade for a year or two, and they didn't speak but only kind of grunted. They had an Indian woman with them who they ordered around with their gruntin' talk. We had some supper and afterwards one of 'em pulled out a bottle of whisky. They got pretty lively, then one of 'em went over to where the Indian gal was sitting out of the firelight and starts draggin' her off into the dark. I got up and the other trapper he tells me to mind my own business, but I hit him across the face and went after the other one. I found 'em and he was just fit to be tied. I gave him a pretty good fight, but he was a big one, and he was drunk. We was in a tangle when I felt a thump, and the other trapper had come up behind and damn near stove in my head with a rifle butt. Just then a shot rang out and the boy I was fightin' just kind of slumped and pulled me down. Then another bullet went over my head and got the other one. The Indian gal had grabbed my feller's gun when we was fightin'. There was enough dead bodies on them plains, and I didn't much want to be part of any more killin', but it was done. The Indian gal was a Sioux, and she didn't show nothin' but pleasure that those two was dead.

In the mornin' we rode out after sort of buryin' the trappers. I knew the wolves would get 'em soon enough though. The Indian had been picked up by those two when she got lost from her family. There'd been a fight and she'd run off and them two had got her and rode off. She'd been with 'em a week or more. I figured we'd better try to find her people, but with the army after 'em, things might be a little hot. I thought maybe we'd cross the line into Canada where she'd be safer and might run into some of her own people. So we turned north.

I kept thinkin' as we rode along, all this land. Hell, there was space for the Indians and the white men and all the rest of the world besides. Why'd we have to kill each other over it. But I couldn't help but come back to it. It was the whites after the Indians every time. The Indians would have been alright if they was just left alone. I knew I wasn't no good white man at all, but I didn't much care. I didn't never really belong in civilization anyway.

We was gettin' up into the Crazy Mountains when trouble hit. We seen signs of camp and Blue Winged Bird - that was the Indian gal's name - she thought it was probably her people. She knew they'd be trackin' the ones that kidnapped her and she figured that once they'd got shut of the cavalry they'd head back down towards the plains where they'd been. We followed them tracks back down along the edge of the mountains, and then we come upon a terrible sight.

It was her people all right, and they'd run smack dab into a cavalry troop headin' north. There wasn't a single one of 'em left alive, not a man or a woman or a child, bout twenty-five or so. Blue Winged Bird, she ran from one to the other of them, just like a crazy person, turnin' 'em over and lookin' at their poor dead faces, and just screamin' and cryin'. She commenced to tearin' her hair and wailin' and I thought she would do herself harm, and I think she might've, but then we hear a noise, like a whimperin' of some little animal. We both looked and over near the trees we see somethin'. She ran over there and there was never such cries of joy. There was a child, one of theirs, and it was her own little boy, who had got overlooked by them murderin' fiends. He couldn't a been much more than four, and he was damn near starved, but he was alright.

She took him up in her arms and out of that terrible place, and I built a fire and we got him warm and got some food into him, and pretty soon he was sleepin' in his mother's arms. When he was good and asleep, she wrapped him up in a blanket I had, and went back among those dead. She told me to stay with him. After awhile I heard some singing and chantin', then it went quiet. She came back. I knowed she'd done what buryin' ceremonies she could for them, and that was important to Indians or they'd never get to their heaven. After while the little boy woke up and looked at me kind of wild eyed, but his mother told him somethin' and he settled down. We stayed there that night and in the morning we headed out. Wasn't no good goin' north with that cavalry goin' that way, so we headed south and west, towards the Yellowstone.

The way westward wasn't too rough till we got in the Rockies, and then it was pretty hard goin'. Bein' summer, we was almost et up by flies and skeeters, but at least it wasn't cold. I had heard about the Yellowstone, but I'd never been there. The gov'ment made it parkland, but wasn't good for much else anyway. Ever' time you kick over a rock a jet of steam like a kettle boilin' over like to scald your toes. I never seen anything like it. One place we got to, it was like a big wide river, but it was all a river of boilin' mud. And that geyser they call Old Faithful just explodin' about once an hour. I never seen such a place. There were some folks there but we steered clear of 'em mainly and come down the other side into Idaho country.

I didn't know rightly what to do. I wanted to get that Indian gal back to her people, but most of 'em was dead, or would be soon. I didn't want to ride up into the middle of the US Cavalry, nohow, with that gal and her boy. I knew what might happen. So we had to steer clear. And I got to say it, too. I had feelings for her, and I know she had some feelings for me too, once we was out of danger. We spent a couple of months like that, just ridin' easy through that beautiful country in Idaho and then down into Wyoming, stayin' near the mountains, lots of game, nice little rivers to swim in when it got hot, not a worry in the world until the weather changed, but that seemed a long way off.

I don't know how it is when you feel happy, you're in the middle of it and you feel like it ain't never goin' to end, and time sort of stops, then you wake up one mornin' and it's over. That's how it was for us. I woke up one mornin' to see some of the meanest lookin' braves standin' around me pointin' rifles, and Bird just screamin' at 'em tellin' 'em how I'd saved her and the boy. They was Sioux, so they'd heard about me, and they wasn't goin' to kill me, but they wasn't going to leave Blue Winged Bird with me neither. They mounted up and her and the boy behind two of 'em, and just like that, they was gone. She looked back at me, but I knew it wasn't no good. She couldn't fight her people, and I sure couldn't. So I set off.

I'd been gone a good spell and I thought maybe I'd go back to Arkansas and se how my Ruthie was, and how big my grandchildren were. So I set off east, through Wyoming, down towards Kansas. Didn't much happen on that trip. It was gettin' on towards winter, October by then, and the plains had that lonesome feel round about sunset when you ride along and feel like you're the only person in the world, and the lonesomest. There was settlers comin' in too, like anything. There was easterners, and there was Europeans too. I passed white people speakin' languages that sounded like nothin' I'd ever heard before, big fair haired folks with blue eyes. They didn't look like the kind of people meant to be out on the prairies with wagons, but they kept comin', hundreds of 'em I saw. I headed down towards Kansas. Frost was just comin' in the air, and all them people on the road and headin' into winter.

I'd been through Kansas before, and it's part of the South, and right next to Missouri, so I felt like I was gettin' near home. I had criss-crossed the country so many times that by now I felt like I knew pret' near every byway and road. I passed through a place in Kansas called Nicodemus. There was a whole bunch of niggers there that was settin' up a place for all the old slaves to come. They called themselves "exodusters" like from the Bible and the exodus of the Jews. I stayed round there a couple of days and who should I meet but my old nigger Jim, who I'd help to run away all those years ago. Jim was just about as glad to see me as I was to see him, which was like sayin' we just fell on each other and all the other niggers around was amazed 'cause they'd never seen no white man and nigger as good friends as me and Jim was. I asked him what he was doin' there and how come he'd left Missouri where he'd lived all his life. He told me he couldn't stand it in Missouri no more, and that after the war and the Emancipation things had got worse for the niggers. He said it was cause the whites were afraid of the niggers, afraid they'd take vengeance on 'em for what they'd done to 'em all those years. But the

Klu Klux Klan was up and ridin', and there'd been lynchins'. One of Jim's boys had got in some trouble with a white farmer and the Klan boys had come round makin' threats, so Jim and his family they all packed up and left for Kansas.

I could hardly believe things had got that bad in Missouri, but then, I don't know why it surprised me. I seen the worst that people can do to each other, you just don't expect it to happen where you grew up and remember what it was like to be a child.

Them exodusters was havin' a pretty rough time. They didn't have hardly any houses built yet, and the prairie hadn't never been plowed round that way. So I stayed around a while and helped Jim how I could. We got his house up and got a barn built. It was too late in the year for gettin' in a crop, but we got the fields plowed and turned and we dug a well. It was all goin' as good as could be when one day round about Christmas time when a couple of rough lookin' white men come ridin' up to where Jim and me was layin' out some fence posts.

"What you doin' here livin' with niggers?" one says and spits so it just misses my shoe.

"I guess it ain't no one's business but mine what I do and who I live with," I says.

"Well, it ain't goin' to be too good for them or their children you keep hangin' around here," the other one says, lookin' evil.

I walked away from Jim a ways and spoke to that pair of lowdowns. "You mean to say you'll bother these folks cause I'm helpin' them out?"

"We do," one says, and kind of smiles. "We don't mind these niggers plowin' up this godforsaken bit of shit-useless land, but no white man's goin' to do it with 'em."

"If I leave, you'll leave them alone?"

"That's the size of it."

I didn't know if I could believe those rogues, but I didn't see how I had no choice, so the next mornin' I packed up and was on my way. I saw them two as I rode up the road, watchin'. One kind of tipped his hat to me as I rode along and I spat in the road. The more I saw of life in America, the more wrong it all seemed to me. Wasn't nothin' fair nor nothin' right. All that beautiful country and all that hope people had, and wasn't nothin' people touched - leastaways white people - that didn't turn bad.

And that wasn't the worst. I got down to Missouri and I caught a boat down to Arkansas. When I got to my old farm wasn't nothin' there. The farmhouse had burned to the ground and the fields gone wild. I looked for the family and finally found Ruthie's husband up country with his parents. There had been a diphtheria epidemic and my Ruthie and her children were all in the ground. He'd just about died himself, but he was gettin' better. He looked like a ghost, but he was young, and he might come back to life. As for me, I might as well have been dead.

Chapter Eight

I drifted. Wasn't no where to hang on to for very long, so I drifted from Arkansas to Louisiana, Louisiana to Texas, Texas down into Mexico then back up again. After a couple of years of livin' like a vagrant and workin' when I could, stealin' when I couldn't, I pitched up in New Mexico, Lincoln County.

Things were pretty hot in Mew Mexico, and I don't just mean the weather. There was a kind of war goin' on between a couple of sets of crooks, Tunstall and Chisum, and those others, Riley, Murphy and Dolan. Riley and his boys had had control of the place and was doin' all manner of things, includin' rustling Chisum's cattle, till Tunstall, an Englishman, come in. He looked pretty good at first, but then he got up to the same kind of tricks as the others. Thing was, the state was just being incorporated, so there was the kind of free space that just lets in trouble. When I'd been there a few days and figured out what was happening, I'd put my money on Dolan and Murphy and Riley - they was meaner. But Tunstall's gang had Billy the Kid fightin' for them, and Billy wasn't all bad. He'd been to school and spoke real well, and he wasn't no vicious killer like they all made out afterwards. Everyone knows Pat Garrett shot him while he was asleep and then turned the whole thing into one big tall story. That's what begun to bother me in those days. You could hear about something happening or someone, then you'd find out the "killer" was just some farm boy, or the "massacre" wasn't nothin' of the kind. Real things turned into stories before they even finished happening, and that's what give people the wrong idea about them. Trouble was, the West got so full of the idea of itself that couldn't nothin' be just what it was. Anyway, I stuck around for awhile, then things hotted up and there was a lot of killing. Billy got out of it and went back to cowboying, rustling mainly, and I went with him. He tried to get a pardon and the governor of the state said he would, then he didn't, and Billy just didn't have no choice. He was a young lad, only twenty-one when Garrett shot him, and in some ways he reminded me of Tom. We had some fine times, out there on the plains of New Mexico and Texas. The country out there was wild and lonesome, and when I was out under the stars at night sometimes I didn't feel so bad about the things that had happened to me and the people that had died. Sometimes I got to wondering why everyone I loved had died and I just kept goin' on like somethin' that can't die. I'd seen too much, that was it, but I didn't feel so bad when I was alone and listening to the wind howl and the cattle lowing out there at night. I guess the world was lonelier than me, and I felt comforted. I think I could've stuck it for awhile, but the law, which wasn't much more than a bunch of rustlers turned lawmen themselves, found out where Billy was laid up and got him. I would have been with him that day he rode over to Pete Maxwell's place at Fort Sumner, but something mighty strange had happened, and I was layin' low, figuring out what I'd better do.

Thing was, I'd seen Tom. First I thought I had to be wrong, I'd seen him fall at the Greasy Grass. But then I remembered, I hadn't seen him dead, just down. The fightin' was hot where he was, and something might have got in the way of that brave and his knife. I didn't see how Tom could've got away, and I wondered at first if I'd seen a ghost, but there was no doubt. It was Tom. This is how it happened. I was down in Roswell, scoutin' out where cattle was moving. No one knew I was with Billy, so I could move around pretty free. I went into the saloon and I saw a bunch of swells - cattlemen, all dressed up. The big boys who ran the show and was pushing all the small ranchers out. I knew most of them by sight, though they wouldn't have paid much attention to an old cowboy like me. I went up to the bar and I looked in the mirror and I seen him. He was smoking a cigar and drinking whiskey at a table with a few of them. Dolan and Riley was there and they were all talking quiet about something. Tom had a big scar down the side of his face, and he looked, well he looked different. Everyone gets older, it wasn't that. It's just that Tom had always been playing at life. It was a game to him. He was just a boy looking for adventures, and really never meant no harm. But now he was different. He didn't look like he didn't mean no harm. He looked like harm was something he took in his stride, like he had an excuse for it. He kind of smiled and said something then looked over toward the bar. I ducked my head. I didn't want him to see me, but it was too late. He looked, and his face kind of changed, like wax in the sun, and just for a minute I seen the old Tom looking out at me. He jumped up and came over. He was glad to see me, that was sure. He sat down and we talked about old times, and how he'd got away from the Greasy Grass - the brave who'd been about to kill him got it first from a rifle shot and Tom had kind of rolled out of the way. He fell in with the end of Benton's troop later - they was the only ones survived, and he lived. He'd been knocking around Texas and New Mexico for a couple of years, and then he'd fell in with this lot. Tom always was one with an eye for the main chance, and he'd found it. He'd got himself a spread out of the corporation and was runnin' cattle on it. I didn't ask too close what his part in it was, cause really I didn't want to know. He looked at me real close and said,

"My friends over there think you're with the Kid. That true Huck?" I could see the others looking over my way so I just said no, that I'd known the Kid, but I was just lookin for something to do now. Then Tom he clapped me on the back and said,

"Fine! You come along with me then Huck, just like old times."

So I made my excuses to go round up my stuff and see some people, and so it happened that I wasn't at our camp when Billy took off. I didn't have no intention of working with Tom and that gang of thieves, but when I heard Billy was dead anyway, I went along. I didn't really know what I'd do, but it was just that by then I'd got nowhere to go, and no one in the world, and here was Tom, my oldest friend, risen from the dead, so I went.

Tom's spread was fine, I'll tell you. Looked like about four or five little ranches had been put together to make one big one. Tom's house had been built by one of the ranchers had been run off by the big boys. I didn't like that much, and I told Tom so. Well, Tom's answer was smooth. Tom always was smooth and always had an answer for everything. He just said that he hadn't done anything to the rancher, the house was empty when he got to it, and it was wasteful to let it all go wild. I still didn't like it, but I had no answer for Tom. That's the trouble. Sometimes you know you're right, but you got no answer for them smooth talkers, and you just end up looking foolish.

At first it was fine, cowboying for Tom's outfit - there was about ten of us working there. We'd work the cattle and put up fences and do all the things necessary on a ranch. At night we'd sit by the fire outside if we was out on the range, or we'd sit around in the bunkhouse and play cards. I'd go talk to Tom in his house, but I was happy sleepin' out in the bunkhouse with the cowboys. But then it changed. There was another rancher had held out against Dolan and Riley's gang. He was up in a little valley in the hills behind our place. He just had a couple hundred head of cattle and wasn't no threat as far as I could see, but Tom said he had to go. It was the principle, he said. He wanted all the land and all the cattle round there to belong to him, as far as he could see. He said he'd give the rancher a fair price and that it was just the American way of business. I told Tom it was just greed and if he continued that way I'd have no more to do with him. He looked at me funny. Thing was, to Tom, it was still just a game. Sufferin' and death and all - it was like it didn't really touch him. Like somewhere part of his heart was missing. He was playing like a boy, and like a boy, he wanted to win. The next morning him and the others set off to tell Cooper to go, I stayed behind. I packed my bedroll and got on my horse and set off in the other direction. I didn't want no more to do with American business if that was the way people acted. Even my best friend Tom was changed by being able to take what he wanted. Ain't nothin' wrong with not gettin' everything you want ever' time you want it. I'd been a farmer and I knew how hard the little man had to work. Then the big boys come in and just take it all. I wanted to do somethin' to stop Tom, but I couldn't, and I felt helpless. As I was ridin' away, I saw about ten more fellas coming up the road, hell for leather. They was just like a little cloud of dust in the distance, then they got bigger and bigger, and when I saw they wasn't going to stop, I took my horse down off the roadway and let them go by. I seen them, and they saw me, and one or two looked at me like they know'd me. They was all fellas who'd farmed or ranched around there, the ones been knocked out by Tom's crew. They all looked mean, and they all looked mad. They was all carrying rifles on their saddles. I thought to myself that maybe this time Tom's luck wasn't goin' to hold out. But I kept ridin'.

Chapter Nine

There wasn't no place to go to escape how bad people behaved toward each other. I thought about goin' down to Mexico but I knew it was just a dream to think people would be any different down there. I'd been down there and I'd seen how bad the peasants was treated. Why, even America was better than that, I thought, but then I remembered all them niggers at Nicodemus, and how the whites just treated them like dirt. And the Sioux. I'd been with the Indians enough to know they had a reason to fight back like they did. The only good people I knew seemed to all be dead, or as good as. It was the year 1879, and I was coming up for fifty years old soon, close as I could reckon.

Seemed like before when things didn't work out, a fella could just light out. When I was a boy, I used to dream of those territories, empty of everythin' but animals and Indians. At least that's what I thought until I got to know what really went on. The Indians, they'd lived in those places for centuries, not doin' no harm, then along comes the whites and just goes bustin' everythin' up. All that beautiful country, enough for everybody, but some people just feel like it's got to be theirs. So there ain't no frontier, and there never was. There was a place that hadn't been looked at like dollars and cents, that's all.

I wandered around again after I left Tom's. People was all up in arms about one thing or another. Some was worried about statehood, some was worried about the Indians. Lots was worried that there wasn't goin' to be no more free land and that the country was all used up. Me, I was just worried about stayin' alive and comfortable, and causin' as little harm as possible. That seemed to me to be as good a goal as any other.

The next few years I just worked doin' whatever I could. I cowboyed when there was cowboyin' to be done; I worked alongside farmers in their fields; I even worked in a saloon in Tombstone for a spell, but that got a little rough so I lit out. It got little bit lonesome, and it got sad sometimes, specially when those times of year come round when I'd lost the people I'd loved. But I held on. There wasn't much choice was there? I ain't never been one for givin' up, but sometimes I wondered what it was all worth, I admit it. I tried to do as little harm and any good I could. I stayed with one homesteading farmer and his family for near enough a year till I reckoned they was on their feet. Then I lit out. The year 1885 found me up in Wyoming. It was still a rough place up there, but nothin' to what it had been a few years before. Well, it happened that Bill Cody was comin' through town, looking for riders to be in his next show. Word was he'd got Sitting Bull riding with him, but I couldn't hardly believe that. I did know there was a good number of Sioux riding with him, and I had a hankering to see some of my old friends, so when he asked me if I'd join the show, I said I would, not havin' any other plans and not havin' anyone expectin' me to come back anywhere. He was takin' the show to Europe, and I liked the idea of being out on the sea again. So we all packed up and headed East.

I'd never been to the East before, like Tom had. We took the railroad all the way to New York where there was a ship waitin' for us. We had a day or two before she sailed, so I looked around the town a bit. I'd never seen so many people rushin' around, 'cept maybe at the Greasy Grass. And ever' one of 'em dressed up like they was goin' to a party. I reckon I looked a mite out of place, but no one seemed to notice. The last day we were there I wandered down to a place called the Five Points, and that was a lot more like the West than anywhere I'd seen. There was gangs of fellas all dressed more or less alike, swaggerin' around. A couple of 'em came up to me and started some sass but I just walked away. I didn't want no trouble. When I got back down to the docks we were just about ready to sail. Ever' body got aboard. we was sailin' at first light. The cowboys and Miss Annie Oakley were all happy to be headin' off, but the Indians did look sick. Sittin' Bull just sat in the front of the boat all night lookin' out, and when we cast off he grabbed the side of the gunnel and looked most as scared as if he'd heard Custer himself was comin' back from the dead to come with us. Not that Sittin' Bull was ever scared of Custer, but Indians don't like spirits of their enemies comin' back at them. Who would?

Well that journey, it was fine. I was glad to be on ship again, and I figured when the Wild West Show was finished, maybe I'd sign on as a sailor again. I liked that life.

When we finally got to London, England, that was something. I never seen such a place. Big and dirty and full of smoke, and all the people running round with their heads down lookin' miserable. There was some big parks though, and I liked that. The show was packed, night after night. Sometimes afterwards people would come up to us and ask us what it was like "out West" and show us things like those lying railroad papers tryin' to get folks to emigrate to some godforsaken bit of Wyoming or someplace just as desolate. But seein' how they lived there in London, I wasn't sure they wouldn't be better off in sod houses in Wyoming than in those piled up, rat-infested places they did live.

I was a cavalry man in the Battle of the Little Bighorn show. It was strange to see Sitting Bull actin' what he'd done ten years afore. It was more than strange, it was like real life had become somethin' else, like it was a picture show, and not real at all. There's something wrong when life turns into a picture show like that. The Indians, they knew it. They wasn't comfortable acting out what they'd been. Neither was I, but I did it. I figured there wasn't no harm givin' people a show, but then I begun to wonder. I wondered if giving them a show didn't make them think that life was somethin' else than what it was, and then make them feel sorry they had the life they did. I was at that battle. I saw the blood and the screamin', and the squaws cutting apart men still alive afterwards, and I seen that field of Blue Winged Bird's dead children. I know it ain't pretty, it's something else altogether. I ain't got the words for it, but I know that makin' it into a show does dishonor to the dead, and to the livin' too. When those poor, pale people would come up to me afterwards with their faces shinin' and asking what the West was like, I thought, well, they can have their dreams. But now I ain't so sure. I ain't sure at all.

We was over in Europe for a spell, doin' our show in those big, dark cities. Sometimes people would come who were real Kings and Dukes, not like the lot I'd known. They didn't seem much diff'rent to me than ordinary folks, only a mite better dressed. It made me feel sick to see Bill and some of the others fawning all over them. Me, I just kept out of the way. I got pretty homesick at times, so I was glad when we packed up our gear and got back on that ship. We had a rough crossing goin' back, and it was hard on the horses. I was never gladder to see anyplace than New York when we come heavin' through that grey sea under a grey sky one morning in October 1886. Once we was back in New York Bill was goin' to do more shows, but I just packed my things and got the first train goin' West. I'd seen enough.

I was near enough fifty-seven years old by then, and I begun to wonder if I was goin' to spend the rest of my life like I had been those last few years, just wandering and ramblin'. It didn't have no appeal no more, but with all my kin dead, and most of my old friends, I didn't know where to go. I figured I might head for Nicodemus and see if Jim was still alive. By now those folks would have settled in, and I didn't think there'd be no more trouble with those rough boys I'd met before. It'd been nearly eleven years since I'd seen Jim, and I thought that was the best thing I could do. On my way out there though, that plan got changed.

You see, I found Tom again, or he found me, whichever way you look at it our paths were goin' to cross forever. I hadn't seen Tom in seven years. When I ran up into him in the dining car of that train, somewhere in the middle of Ohio, he looked as happy as he could be, and just for a second, I saw the old Tom again. It always made me sad when that happened. I'd've rather that ghost stayed buried, 'cause there wasn't none of the old boy left in the man, 'cept once in a while that flicker in his eyes. He was quite a swell, and he told me that he'd gone into politics. He'd made a packet of money in New

Mexico off the backs of those ranchers they'd driven out. That day I left he had high-tailed it when that gang arrived, but he got back and in the end it was the small people that paid, just like always. He was on his way back from Washington to New Mexico. He was full of talk about dams and irrigation and how the whole Southwest was goin' to flower like Canaan in the desert. I think he almost believed it. He'd seen someone called Gilpin in Washington, and ever' sentence, was, "Gilpin says this, Gilpin says that." I didn't see no harm in trying to make a little farm near a reservoy or a stream, but Tom, he was talkin' about bringin' in thousands of people, changin' the land. I guess I just thought the land was alright like it was. When I asked him where all the rattlesnakes would go, he didn't seem to think it was funny. Anyway, since I had no where in particular to go, I went along with Tom again, back to New Mexico. Tom still had his spread in Lincoln County, and so I settled back in, doing some cowboyin' and jobs around the place. Sometimes I'd eat my dinner with Tom, but sometimes he'd have bigwigs stayin' there, so mostly I just did my work and slept in the bunkhouse. I didn't have no complaints. A couple of years just sort of drifted by, and before I knew it it was nearly 1890, and I was sixty years old.

One evening I was sittin' out by the corral, havin' a smoke and just lookin' at the mountains. Fact was, I was thinkin' about Mary-Jane, and Ruthie, like I sometimes did, and I was feeling a mite sad, but I didn't let it show. Tom he comes out smokin' a big cigar and says to me, "Huck, I got some business in South Dakota comin' up. Do you want to come with me?" Well I jumped at the chance. Fact was I was gettin' itchy feet, but I knew I prob'ly ought to stay where I was, gettin' to be an old man and all. So I says yes, and I never regretted no decision in my life more.

We took the train most of the way, and the stage the last bit. Tom had some business with some other bigwigs up in Helena, and since he was goin' to be more than a week doin' whatever devilment politicians do when they get together, I reckoned I'd look up some of my old friends in the Dakota country. It was November, and gettin' powerful cold already. I bought myself a skin coat and borrowed money from Tom for a horse. Then I set out towards the Sioux country. I got as far as Standing Rock, and who should I meet comin' round a bend in the road but Buffalo Bill Cody! I'd heard he was back in those parts, and one morning we sat in the Indian Agency office and Bill told me the story. He'd been sent for from Chicago to try and talk sense to Sitting Bull. Sitting Bull was back in those parts havin' left the Wild West Show some time before. Now all the Sioux, and all the other Indians in those parts was goin' crazy doin' the Ghost Dance.

I had heard a bit about this dance, but Bill filled me in. It was started by the Paiutes and their leader was an Indian called Wovoka. Wovoka told the Indians that the white men was all going to disappear and be covered by grass and that if the Indians did the Ghost Dance all their dead would come back, and all the buffalo that had been killed. He didn't tell them to go on the warpath, not at all, it was more like what the Widow Douglas used to say about the heavenly reward all good Christians were goin' to get. Only I don't reckon the Widow would a cared much about the buffalo part. But I reckoned the Indians had heard about that stuff from a lot of ladies who thought like the Widow. Anyway, Bill didn't see how they was doin' any harm, and I didn't neither. He'd been sent for to talk sense to Sittin' Bull, who the bigwigs reckoned was the main organizer. Trouble was, the Indian agent in Standing Rock, a fellow called McLaughlin, he thought Bill wasn't up to the job and got Washington to call him back. So Bill hadn't even seen Sitting Bull, and he was pretty disgusted. After he left I thought I might try to find Sitting Bull myself, so late November I set out.

It was cold, bitter cold out there, and I'd got used to a softer life down in New Mexico, but ever' where I went I found bands of Indians, and they always took me in. They was dancin', they was dancin' like crazy, and thinkin' of what they'd suffered, I didn't blame them. I got to thinkin' about all my dead ones, and after a few weeks, I started dancin' too. Some of the old ones they remembered me, and some of the young ones had heard about the Painted Man, so I fitted in. When I finally found Sittin' Bull I knew all I needed to know about the Ghost Dance, and I hoped the Indians would get their dead back, and I hoped I would too. It was December by then, and near enough to Christmas. I'd given up all idea of goin' back with Tom. He must a wondered where I'd got to, but I didn't care. Nothin' seemed to make no difference but what was happening then.

We danced.

In the morning of December 15th, I woke up hearin' noise. I was sleepin' in a teepee near Sittin' Bull's cabin. It was still dark and I looked out and all I could see was shapes. There was some talking, then it went quiet, then I see Sittin' Bull comin' out of his cabin, surrounded by a lot of other Sioux. They wasn't dancers, they was the Indian police, turncoats who worked for the whites. It was hard to see what was happening in the gloom, but I could see there was a ruckus. One of 'em started pullin' at Sitting Bull and he backed off. Then there was a shot , then another. You know what it's like when you see something fallin', and it seems like it's goin' slow, then it just explodes when it hits the ground. That's what them shots were like. Quiet, then all hell. A minute later, the most awful wailing started. By this time more and more of the Ghost Dancers had come round. Someone shouted that Sitting Bull was shot, and right then his old horse, one of the ones from the Wild West Show, started dancin' around, prancin' like he'd done in those tents all over the world. Ever' one just stopped and stared, but the horse shied and ran off and the killin' began. The Indian police would a been wiped out but for a troop of cavalry that rode up. The dancers scattered but I knew there was trouble to come.

Two weeks later I was ridin' with Big Foot up towards Pine Ridge. Big Foot was sick and he rode in a wagon. It was just past Christmas. I knew 'cause we'd passed some white folks on the day who told us. About half way there we ran into the cavalry. They had orders to go with the Indians to the agency, they said, so we was pretty much surrounded by those soldiers, all trampin' through that bitter winter cold. Lots of the Sioux was sick and there was a lot of women and children in that band. We got to a place called Wounded Knee on the evening of December 27th. In the morning the soldiers took all their guns away from the Indians. I hadn't got no guns, and they didn't bother with me anyway, thinkin' I was just some old trapper squaw-man. There was a deaf Indian called Black Coyote who wouldn't give up his gun. There was some trouble with him, and the gun went off. Suddenly the soldiers all started shootin'.

I seen bad things in my life. I seen Gettysburg, I seen the Little Big Horn. But I ain't never seen nothin' like Wounded Knee. Women and children and old men just runnin' ever' where and screamin' and shoutin', and them soldiers, they just kept on shootin'. I don't know why I didn't get hit myself, 'cept my horse he shied and run for the guns which was over us, so I got missed. It went on and on. Finally it stopped and the soldiers they looked around at what they'd done. Some of 'em wasn't too old, but God forgive me I could a wished them dead. They was sort of stunned, then they started actin' like they'd won some battle. I guess they thought since they was the Seventh Cavalry it was the Bighorn all over again. There was a officer up on his horse behind the foot soldiers, and I looked over at him. There was a man by his side, and by God that man was Tom.

Well, I reckoned my life was over then. I knew then that all the goodness that ever was in a person, or in a country, could turn to dust and ashes. Tom, he looked up and he saw me. He looked shocked, then his face kind of twisted, then he turned the other way. I did what I could to help with the wounded and the dead, then I mounted up and left that country. I rode as far away as I could, and I ain't never goin' back.

Epilogue

Well, since that day at Wounded Knee, I've just roamed. I don't have no faith in no one no more, and in no thing in this world. Sometimes I wish I could believe in the Widow's God, but after what I seen, I can't.

There's good people and there's bad people, I know that, but I can't figure how the bad ones always get what they want and the good ones always end up dying, or worse.

What still puzzles me is how Tom could 'a gone so wrong. If there was ever a boy fit to be somethin' special, it was him. Seems like maybe he felt like he was too. If he'd been a nobody like me maybe he'd 'a been alright. Someone said it about festerin' lilies stinkin' worse than weeds, and I know what they mean. It's kind of like this whole country. I been over most of it now, and even now sometimes I look out over a mountain range , or think about the sea, or about all them people workin' so hard and comin' west, and wantin' somethin' better, and for a minute, I think, by jiminy, it is alright! Then I remember Wounded Knee, and the Greasy Grass, and I think about Gettysburg, and those boys diggin' in the mountains, carin' 'bout nothin' but gold. I think about them homesteaders driven out by the big boys, and I think about the land, all tore up with fences, and mines, now dams, they say, all so folks can get rich. If I been lucky, it's been 'cause bein' born poor, I never did develop no taste for money.

I'm goin' to die soon myself, I know that. I'm a old man now, and I've had my time. What I'm goin' to do is find myself a big high mountaintop and just climb up there and watch the sun rise and set, the moon rise, and the stars come out at night. If some bear or wolf eats me, I don't care. I'd rather be part of this earth than part of anything else. That's the only thing I'm sure of anymore, that the stars and the sun and the wind and the rain are more like my friends than anyone livin'. And I find some comfort in that.